D1366638

Sarah H. Bradford

The Extraordinary Life Story of Harriet Tubman

e-artnow 2018

Sarah H. Bradford

The Extraordinary Life Story of Harriet Tubman

e-artnow, 2018
Contact: info@e-artnow.org

ISBN 978-80-268-9131-4

Contents

Scenes in the Life of Harriet Tubman

INTRODUCTION

THE following little story was written by Mrs. Sarah H. Bradford, of Geneva, with the single object of furnishing some help to the subject of the memoir. Harriet Tubman's services and sufferings during the rebellion, which are acknowledged in the letters of Gen. Saxton, and others, it was thought by many, would justify the bestowment of a pension by the Government. But the difficulties in the way of procuring such relief, suggested other methods, and finally the present one. The narrative was prepared on the eve of the author's departure for Europe, where she still remains. It makes no claim whatever to literary merit. Her hope was merely that the considerably numerous public already in part acquainted with Harriet's story, would furnish purchasers enough to secure a little fund for the relief of this remarkable woman. Outside that circle she did not suppose the memoir was likely to meet with much if any sale.

In furtherance of the same benevolent scheme, and in order to secure the whole avails of the work for Harriet's benefit, a subscription has been raised more than sufficient to defray the entire cost of publication. This has been effected by the generous exertions of Wm. G. Wise, Esq., of this city. The whole amount was contributed by citizens of Auburn, with the exception of two liberal subscriptions by Gerrit Smith, Esq., and Mr. Wendell Phillips.

Mr. Wise has also consented, at Mrs. Bradford's request, to act as trustee for Harriet; and will receive, invest, and apply, for her benefit, whatever may accrue from the sale of this book.

The spirited wood-cut likeness of Harriet, in her costume as scout, was furnished by the kindness of Mr. J. C. Darby, of this city.

S. M. H.

AUBURN, Dec. 1, 1868.

PREFACE

IT is proposed in this little book to give a plain and unvarnished account of some scenes and adventures in the life of a woman who, though one of earth's lowly ones, and of dark-hued skin, has shown an amount of heroism in her character rarely possessed by those of any station in life. Her name (we say it advisedly and without exaggeration) deserves to be handed down to posterity side by side with the names of Joan of Arc, Grace Darling, and Florence Nightingale; for not one of these women has shown more courage and power of endurance in facing danger and death to relieve human suffering, than has this woman in her heroic and successful endeavors to reach and save all whom she might of her oppressed and suffering race, and to pilot them from the land of Bondage to the promised land of Liberty. Well has she been called *"Moses,"* for she has been a leader and deliverer unto hundreds of her people.

Worn down by her sufferings and fatigues, her health permanently affected by the cruelties to which she has been subjected, she is still laboring to the utmost limit of her strength for the support of her aged parents, and still also for her afflicted people--by her own efforts supporting two schools for Freedmen at the South, and supplying them with clothes and books; never obtruding herself, never asking for charity, except for "her people."

It is for the purpose of aiding her in ministering to the wants of her aged parents, and in the hope of securing to them the little home which they are in danger of losing from inability to pay the whole amount due--which amount was partly paid when our heroine left them to throw herself into the work of aiding our suffering soldiers--that this little account, drawn from her by persevering endeavor, is given to the friends of humanity.

The writer of this story has till very lately known less personally of the subject of it, than many others to whom she has for years been an object of interest and care. Put through relations and friends in Auburn, and also through Mrs. Commodore Swift of Geneva, and her sisters, who have for many years known and esteemed this wonderful woman, she has heard tales of her deeds of heroism which seemed almost too strange for belief, and were invested with the charm of romance.

During a sojourn of some months in the city of Auburn, while the war was in progress, the writer used to see occasionally in her Sunday-school class the aged mother of Harriet, and also some of those girls who bad been brought from the South by this remarkable woman. She also wrote letters for the old people to commanding officers at the South, making inquiries about Harriet, and received answers telling of her untiring devotion to our wounded and sick soldiers, and of her efficient aid in various ways to the cause of the Union.

By the graphic pen of Mrs. Stowe, the incidents of such a life as that of the subject of this little memoir might be wrought up into a tale of thrilling interest, equaling, if not exceeding, anything in her world-renowned "Uncle Tom's Cabin;" but the story of Harriet Tubman needs not the drapery of fiction; the bare unadorned facts are enough to stir the hearts of the friends of humanity, the friends of liberty, the lovers of their country.

There are those who will sneer, there are those who have already done so, at this *quixotic attempt* to make a heroine of a black woman, and a slave; but it may possibly be that there are some natures, though concealed under fairer skins, who have not the capacity to comprehend such general and self-sacrificing devotion to the cause of others as that here delineated, and therefore they resort to scorn and ridicule, in order to throw discredit upon the whole story.

Much has been left out which would have been highly interesting, because of the impossibility of substantiating by the testimony of others the truth of Harriet's statements. But whenever it has been possible to find those who were cognizant with the facts stated, they have been corroborated in every particular.

A few years hence and we seem to see a gathering where the wrongs of earth will be righted, and Justice, long delayed, will assert itself, and perform its office. Then not a few of those who had esteemed themselves the wise and noble of this world, "will begin with shame to take the lowest place;" while upon Harriet's dark head a kind hand will be placed, and in her ear a gentle voice will sound, saying: "Friend! come up higher!"

S. H. B.

The following letters to the writer from those well-known and distinguished philanthropists, Hon. Gerrit Smith and Wendell Phillips, and one from Frederick Douglass, addressed to Harriet, will serve as the best introduction that can be given of the subject of this memoir to its readers:

Letter from Hon. Gerrit Smith.

PETERBORO, June 13, 1868.

My DEAR MADAME: I am happy to learn that you are to speak to the public of Mrs. Harriet Tubman. Of the remarkable events of her life I have no *personal* knowledge, but of the truth of them as she describes them I have no doubt.

I have often listened to her, in her visits to my family, and I am confident that she is not only truthful, but that she has a rare discernment, and a deep and sublime philanthropy.

With great respect your friend,
GERRIT SMITH.

Letter from Wendell Phillips.

JUNE 16, 1868.

DEAR MADAME: The last time I ever saw John Brown was under my own roof, as he brought Harriet Tubman to me, saying: "Mr. Phillips, I bring you one of the best and bravest persons on this continent--*General* Tubman, as we call her."

He then went on to recount her labors and sacrifices in behalf of her race. After that, Harriet spent some time in Boston, earning the confidence and admiration of all those who were working for freedom. With their aid she went to the South more than once, returning always with a squad of self-emancipated men, women, and children, for whom her marvelous skill had opened the way of escape. After the war broke out, she was sent with indorsements from Governor Andrew and his friends to South Carolina, where in the service of the Nation she rendered most important and efficient aid to our army.

In my opinion there are few captains, perhaps few colonels, who have done more for the loyal cause since the war began, and few men who did before that time more for the colored race, than our fearless and most sagacious friend, Harriet.

Faithfully yours,
WENDELL PHILLIPS.

Letter from Frederick Douglass.

ROCHESTER, August 29, 1868.

DEAR HARRIET: I am glad to know that the story of your eventful life has been written by a kind lady, and that the same is so soon to be published. You ask for what you do not need when you call upon me for a word of commendation. I need such words from you far more than you can need them from me, especially where your superior labors and devotion to the cause of the lately enslaved of our land are known as I know them. The difference between us is very marked. Most that I have done and suffered in the service of our cause has been in public, and I have received much encouragement at every step of the way. You on the other hand have labored in a private way. I have wrought in the day--you in the night. I have had the applause of the crowd and the satisfaction that comes of being approved by the multitude, while the most that you have done has been witnessed by a few trembling, scarred, and foot-sore bondmen and women, whom you have led out of the house of bondage, and whose heartfelt *"God bless you"* has been your only reward. The midnight sky and the silent stars have been the witnesses of your devotion to freedom and of your heroism. Excepting John Brown –of sacred memory--I know of no one who has willingly encountered more perils and hardships to serve our enslaved people than you have. Much that you have done would seem improbable to those who do not know you as I know you. It is to me a great pleasure and a great privilege to bear testimony to your character and your works, and to say to those to whom you may come, that I regard you in every way truthful and trustworthy.

Your friend,
FREDERICK DOUGLASS.

SOME SCENES IN THE LIFE OF HARRIET TUBMAN

HARRIET TUBMAN, known at various times, and in various places, by many different names, such as "Moses," in allusion to her being the leader and guide to so many of her people in their exodus from the Land of Bondage; "the Conductor of the Underground Railroad;" and "Moll Pitcher," for the energy and daring by which she delivered a fugitive slave who was about to be dragged back to the South; was for the first twenty-five years of her life a slave on the eastern shore of Maryland. Her own master she represents as never unnecessarily cruel; but as was common among slaveholders, he often hired out his slaves to others, some of whom proved to be tyrannical and brutal to the utmost limit of their power.

She had worked only as a field-hand for many years, following the oxen, loading and unloading wood, and carrying heavy burdens, by which her naturally remarkable power of muscle was so developed that her feats of strength often called forth the wonder of strong laboring men. Thus was she preparing for the life of hardship and endurance which lay before her, for the deeds of daring she was to do, and of which her ignorant and darkened mind at that time never dreamed.

The first person by whom she was hired was a woman who, though married and the mother of a family, was still "Miss Susan" to her slaves, as is customary at the South. This woman was possessed of the good things of this life, and provided liberally for her slaves--so far as food and clothing went. But she had been brought up to believe, and to act upon the belief, that a slave could be taught to do nothing, and *would* do nothing but under the sting of the whip. Harriet, then a young girl, was taken from her life in the field, and having never seen the inside of a house better than a cabin in the negro quarters, was put to house-work without being told how to do anything. The first thing was to put a parlor in order. "Move these chairs and tables into the middle of the room, sweep the carpet clean, then dust everything, and put them back in their places!" These were the directions given, and Harriet was left alone to do her work. The whip was in sight on the mantel-piece, as a reminder of what was to be expected if the work was not done well. Harriet fixed the furniture as she was told to do, and swept with all her strength, raising a tremendous dust. The moment she had finished sweeping, she took her dusting cloth, and wiped everything "so you could see your face in 'em, de shone so," in haste to go and set the table for breakfast, and do her other work. The dust which she had set flying only settled down again on chairs, tables, and the piano. "Miss Susan" came in and looked around. Then came the call for "Minty"– Harriet's name was Araminta at the South.

She drew her up to the table, saying, "What do you mean by doing my work this way, you--!" and passing her finger on the table and piano, she showed her the mark it made through the dust. "Miss Susan, I done sweep and dust jus' as you tole me." But the whip was already taken down, and the strokes were falling on head and face and neck. Four times this scene was repeated before breakfast, when, during the fifth whipping, the door opened, and "Miss Emily" came in. She was a married sister of "Miss Susan," and was making her a visit, and though brought up with the same associations as her sister, seems to have been a person of more gentle and reasonable nature. Not being able to endure the screams of the child any longer, she came in, took her sister by the arm, and said, "If you do not stop whipping that child, I will leave your house, and never come back!" Miss Susan declared that "she *would* not mind, and she slighted her work on purpose." Miss Emily said, "Leave her to me a few moments;" and Miss Susan left the room, indignant. As soon as they were alone, Miss Emily said: "Now, Minty, show me how you do your work." For the sixth time Harriet removed all the furniture into the middle of the room; then she swept; and the moment she had done sweeping, she took the dusting cloth to wipe off the furniture. "Now stop there," said Miss Emily; "go away now, and do some of your other work, and when it is time to dust, I will call you." When the time came she called her, and explained to her how the dust had now settled, and that if she wiped it off now, the furniture would remain bright and clean. These few words an hour or two before, would have saved Harriet her whippings for that day, as they probably did for many a day after.

While with this woman, after working from early morning till late at night, she was obliged to sit up all night to rock a cross, sick child. Her mistress laid upon her bed with a whip under her pillow, and slept; but if the tired nurse forgot herself for a moment, if her weary head dropped, and her hand ceased to rock the cradle, the child would cry out, and then down would come the whip upon the neck and face of the poor weary creature. The scars are still plainly visible where the whip cut into the flesh. Perhaps her mistress was preparing her, though she did not know it then, by this enforced habit of wakefulness, for the many long nights of travel, when she was the leader and guide of the weary and hunted ones who were escaping from bondage.

"Miss Susan" got tired of Harriet, as Harriet was determined she should do, and so abandoned intention of buying her, and sent her back to her master. She was next hired out to the man who inflicted upon her the lifelong injury from which she is suffering now, by breaking her skull with a weight from the scales. The injury thus inflicted causes her often to fall into a state of somnolency from which it is almost impossible to rouse her. Disabled and sick, her flesh all wasted away, she was returned to her *owner*. He tried to sell her, but no one would buy her. "Dey said dey wouldn't give a sixpence for me," she said.

"And so," she said, "from Christmas till March I worked as I could, and I *prayed* through all the long nights--I groaned and prayed for ole master: 'Oh Lord, convert master!' 'Oh Lord, change dat man's heart!' 'Pears like I prayed all de time," said Harriet; " 'bout my work, everywhere, I prayed an' I groaned to de Lord. When I went to de horse-trough to wash my face, I took up de water in my han' an' I said, 'Oh Lord, wash me, make me clean!' Den I take up something to wipe my face, an' I say, 'Oh Lord, wipe away all my sin!' When I took de broom and began to sweep, I groaned, 'Oh Lord, wha'soebber sin dere be in my heart, sweep it out, Lord, clar an' clean!'" No words can describe the pathos of her tones, as she broke out into these words of prayer, after the manner of her people. "An' so," said she, "I prayed all night long for master, till the first of March; an' all the time he was bringing people to look at me, an' trying to sell me. Den we heard dat some of us was gwine to be sole to go wid de chain-gang down to de cotton an' rice fields, and dey said I was gwine, an' my brudders, an' sisters. Den I changed my prayer. Fust of March I began to pray, 'Oh Lord, if you ant nebber gwine to change dat man's heart, kill him, Lord, an' take him out ob de way.'

"Nex' ting I heard old master was dead, an' he died jus' as he libed. Oh, then, it 'peared like I'd give all de world full ob gold, if I had it, to bring dat poor soul back. But I couldn't pray for him no longer."

The slaves were told that their master's will provided that none of them should be sold out of the State. This satisfied most of them, and they were very happy. But Harriet was not satisfied; she never closed her eyes that she did not imagine she saw the horsemen coming, and heard the screams of women and children, as they were being dragged away to a far worse slavery than that they were enduring there. Harriet was married at this time to a free negro, who not only did not trouble himself about her fears, but did his best to betray her, and bring her back after she escaped. She would start up at night with the cry, "Oh, dey're comin', dey're comin', I mus' go!"

Her husband called her a fool, and said she was like old Cudjo, who when a joke went round, never laughed till half an hour after everybody else got through, and so just as all danger was past she began to be frightened. But still Harriet in fancy saw the horsemen coming, and heard the screams of terrified women and children. "And all that time, in my dreams and visions," she said, "I seemed to see a line, and on the other side of that line were green fields, and lovely flowers, and beautiful white ladies, who stretched out their arms to me over the line, but I couldn't reach them nohow. I always fell before I got to the line."

One Saturday it was whispered in the quarters that two of Harriet's sisters had been sent off with the chain-gang. That morning she started, having persuaded three of her brothers to accompany her, but they had not gone far when the brothers, appalled by the dangers before and behind them, determined to go back, and in spite of her remonstrances dragged her with them. In fear and terror, she remained over Sunday, and on Monday night a negro from another part of the plantation came privately to tell Harriet that herself and brothers were to be carried off that night. The poor old mother, who belonged to the same mistress, was just going to milk. Harriet wanted to get away without letting her know, because she knew that she would raise an uproar and prevent her going, or insist upon going with her, and the time for this was not yet. But she must give some intimation to those she was going to leave of her intention, and send such a farewell as she might to the friends and relations on the plantation. Those communications were generally made by singing. They sang as they walked along the country roads, and the chorus was taken up by others, and the uninitiated knew not the hidden meaning of the words--

> When dat ar ole chariot comes,
> I'm gwine to lebe you;
> I'm boun' for de promised land,
> I'm gwine to lebe you.

These words meant something more than a journey to the Heavenly Canaan. Harriet said, "Here, mother, go 'long; I'll do the milkin' to-night and bring it in." The old woman went to her cabin. Harriet took down her sun-bonnet, and went on to the "big house," where some of her relatives lived as house servants. She thought she could trust Mary, but there were others in the kitchen, and she could say nothing. Mary began to frolic with her. She threw her across the kitchen, and ran out, knowing that Mary would follow her. But just as they turned the corner of the house, the master to whom Harriet was now hired, came riding up on his horse. Mary darted back, and Harriet thought there was no way now but to sing. But "the Doctor," as the master was called, was regarded with special awe by his slaves; if they were singing or talking together in the field, or on the road, and "the Doctor" appeared, all was hushed till he passed. But Harriet had no time for ceremony; her friends must have a warning; and whether the Doctor thought her *"imperent"* or not, she must sing him farewell. So on she went to meet him, singing:

> I'm sorry I'm gwine to lebe you,
> Farewell, oh farewell;
> But I'll meet you in the mornin',
> Farewell, oh farewell.

The Doctor passed, and she bowed as she went on, still singing:

> I'll meet you in the mornin',
> I'm boun' for de promised land,
> On the oder side of Jordan,
> Boun' for de promised land.

She reached the gate and looked round; the Doctor had stopped his horse, and had turned around in the saddle, and was looking at her as if there might be more in this than "met the ear." Harriet closed the gate, went on a little way, came back, the Doctor still gazing at her. She lifted up the gate as if she had not latched it properly, waved her hand to him, and burst out again:

> I'll meet you in the mornin',
> Safe in de promised land,
> On the oder side of Jordan,
> Boun' for de promised land.

And she started on her journey, "not knowing whither she went," except that she was going to follow the north star, till it led her to liberty. Cautiously and by night she traveled, cunningly feeling her way, and finding out who were friends; till after a long and painful journey she found, in answer to careful inquiries, that she had at last crossed that magic "line" which then separated the land of bondage from the land of freedom; for this was before *we* were commanded by law to take part in the iniquity of slavery, and aid in taking and sending back those poor hunted fugitives who had manhood and intelligence enough to enable them to make their way thus far towards freedom.

"When I found I had crossed dat *line*," she said, "I looked at my hands to see if I was de same pusson. There was such a glory ober ebery ting; de sun came like gold through the trees, and ober the fields, and I felt like I was in Heaben."

But then came the bitter drop in the cup of joy. She said she felt like a man who was put in State Prison for twenty-five years. All these twenty-five years he was thinking of his home, and longing for the time when he would see it again. At last the day comes--he leaves the prison gates--he makes his way to his old home, but his old home is not there. The house has been pulled down, and a new one has been put up in its place; his family and friends are gone nobody knows where; there is no one to take him by the hand, no one to welcome him.

"So it was with me," she said. "I had crossed the line. I was *free;* but there was no one to welcome me to the land of freedom. I was a stranger in a strange land; and my home, after all, was down in Maryland; because my father, my mother, my brothers, and sisters, and friends were there. But I was free, and *they* should be free. I would make a home in the North and bring them there, God helping me. Oh, how I prayed then," she said; "I said to de Lord, 'I'm gwine to hole stiddy on to *you,* an' I *know* you'll see me through.'"

She came to Philadelphia, and worked in hotels, in club houses, and afterwards at Cape May. Whenever she had raised money enough to pay expenses, she would make her way back, hide herself, and in various ways give notice to those who were ready to strike for freedom. When her party was made up, they would start always on Saturday night, because advertisements could not be sent out on Sunday, which gave them one day in advance.

Then the pursuers would start after them. Advertisements would be posted everywhere. There was one reward of $12,000 offered for the head of the woman who was constantly appearing and enticing away parties of slaves from their master. She had traveled in the cars when these posters were put up over her head, and she heard them read by those about her--for she could not read herself. Fearlessly she went on, trusting in the Lord. She said, "I started with this idea in my head, 'Dere's *two* things I've got a *right* to, and dese are, Death or Liberty--one or tother I mean to have. No one will take me back alive; I shall fight for my liberty, and when de time has come for me to go, de Lord will let dem kill me." And acting upon this simple creed, and firm in this trusting faith, she went back and forth *nineteen times,* according to the reckoning of her friends. She remembers that she went eleven times from Canada, but of the other journeys she kept no reckoning.

While Harriet was working as cook in one of the large hotels in Philadelphia, the play of "Uncle Tom's Cabin" was being performed for many weeks every night. Some of her fellow-servants wanted her to I go and see it. "No," said Harriet, "I haint got no heart to go and see the sufferings of my people played on de stage. I've heard 'Uncle Tom's Cabin' read, and I tell you Mrs Stowe's pen hasn't begun to paint what slavery is as I have seen it at the far South. I've seen de *real ting,* and I don't want to see it on no stage or in no teater."

I will give here an article from a paper published nearly a year ago, which mentions that the price set upon the head of Harriet was much higher than I have stated it to be. When asked about this, Harriet said she did not know whether it was so, but she heard them read from one paper that the reward offered was $12,000.

"Among American women," says the article referred to, "who has shown a courage and self-devotion to the welfare of others, equal to Harriet Tubman? Hear her story of going down again and again into the very jaws of slavery, to rescue her suffering people, bringing them off through perils and dangers enough to appall the stoutest heart, till she was known among them as 'Moses.'

"*Forty thousand dollars* was not too great a reward for the Maryland slaveholders to offer for her.

"Think of her brave spirit, as strong as Daniel's of old, in its fearless purpose to serve God, even though the fiery furnace should be her portion. I have looked into her dark face, and wondered and admired as I listened to the thrilling deeds her lion heart had prompted her to dare. 'I have heard their groans and sighs, and seen their tears, and I would give every drop of blood in my veins to free them,' she said.

"The other day, at Gerrit Smith's, I saw this heroic woman, whom the pen of genius will yet make famous, as one of the noblest Christian hearts ever inspired to lift the burdens of the wronged and oppressed, and what do you think she said to me? She had been tending and caring for our Union black (and white) soldiers in hospital during the war, and at the end of her labors was on her way home, coming in a car through New Jersey. A white man, the conductor, thrust her out of the car with such violence that she has not been able to work scarcely any since; and as she told me of the pain she had and still suffered, she said she did not know what she should have done for herself, and the old father and mother she takes care of, if Mr. Wendell Phillips had not sent her $60, that kept them warm through the winter. She had a letter from W. H. Seward to Maj.-Gen. Hunter, in which he says, 'I have known her long, and a nobler, higher spirit, or truer, seldom dwells in the human form.'"

It will be impossible to give any connected account of the different journeys taken by Harriet for the rescue of her people, as she herself has no idea of the dates connected with them, or of the order in which they were made. She thinks she was about 25 when she made her own escape, and this was in the last year of James K. Polk's administration. From that time till the beginning of the war, her years were spent in these journeyings back and forth, with intervals between, in which she worked only to spend the avails of her labor in providing for the wants of her next party of fugitives. By night she traveled, many times on foot, over mountains, through forests, across rivers, mid perils by land, perils by water, perils from enemies, "perils among false brethren." Sometimes members of her party would become exhausted, foot-sore, and bleeding, and declare they could not go on, they must stay where they dropped down, and die; others would think a voluntary return to slavery better than being overtaken and carried back, and would insist upon returning; then there was no remedy but force; the revolver carried by this bold and daring pioneer would be pointed at their heads. "Dead niggers tell no tales," said Harriet; "Go on or die;" and so she compelled them to drag their weary limbs on their northward journey.

At one time she collected and sent on a gang of thirty-nine fugitives in the care of others, as from some cause she was prevented from accompanying them. Sometimes, when she and her party were concealed in the woods, they saw their pursuers pass, on their horses, down the high road, tacking up the advertisements for them on the fences and trees.

"And den how we laughed," said she. "*We* was de fools, and *dey* was de wise men; but we wasn't fools enough to go down de high road in de broad daylight." At one time she left her party in the woods, and went by a long and roundabout way to one of the "stations of the Underground Railway," as she called them. Here she procured food for her famished party, often paying out of her hardly-gained earnings, five dollars a day for food for them. But she dared not go back to them till night, for fear of being watched, and thus revealing their hiding-place. After nightfall, the sound of a hymn sung at a distance comes upon the ears of the concealed and famished fugitives in the woods, and they know that their deliverer is at hand. They listen eagerly for the words she sings, for by them they are to be warned of danger, or informed of safety. Nearer and nearer comes the unseen singer, and the words are wafted to their ears:

Hail, oh hail ye happy spirits,
Death no more shall make you fear,

No grief nor sorrow, pain nor anger (anguish)
Shall no more distress you there.

Around him are ten thousan' angels,
Always ready to 'bey comman'.
Dey are always hobring round you,
Till you reach the hebbenly lan'.

Jesus, Jesus will go wid you;
He will lead you to his throne;
He who died has gone before you,
Trod de wine-press all alone.

He whose thunders shake creation;
He who bids the planets roll;
He who rides upon the temple, (tempest)
An' his scepter sways de whole.

Dark and thorny is de desert,
Through de pilgrim makes his ways,
Yet beyon' dis vale of sorrow,
Lies de fiel's of endless days.

I give these words exactly as Harriet sang them to me to a sweet and simple Methodist air. "De first time I go by singing dis hymn, dey don't come out to me," she said, "till I listen if de coast is clar; den when I go back and sing it again, dey come out. But if I sing:

Moses go down in Egypt,
Till ole Pharo' let me go;
Hadn't been for Adam's fall,
Shouldn't hab to died at all,
den dey don't come out, for dere's danger in de way."

And so by night travel, by hiding, by signals, by threatening, she brought the people safely to the land of liberty. But after the passage of the Fugitive Slave law, she said, "I wouldn't trust Uncle Sam wid my people no longer; I brought 'em all clar off to Canada."

Of the very many interesting stories told me by Harriet, I cannot refrain from telling to my readers that of *Joe,* who accompanied her upon her seventh or eighth journey from Maryland to Canada.

Joe was a noble specimen of a negro, and was hired out by his master to a man for whom he worked faithfully for six years, saving him the expense of an overseer, and taking all trouble off his hands. At length this man found him so absolutely necessary to him, that he determined to buy him at any cost. His master held him proportionably high. However, by paying a thousand dollars down for him, and promising to pay another thousand in a certain time, Joe passed into the hands of his new master.

As may be imagined, Joe was somewhat surprised when the first order issued from his master's lips, was, "Now, Joe, strip and take a whipping!" Joe's experience of *whippings,* as he had seen them inflicted upon others, was not such as to cause him particularly to desire to go through the same operation on his own account; and he, naturally enough, demurred, and at first thought of resisting. But he called to mind a scene which he had witnessed a few days before, in the field, the particulars of which are too horrible and too harassing to the feelings to be given to my readers, and he thought it best to submit; but first he tried remonstrance.

"Mas'r," said he, "habn't I always been faithful to you? Habn't I worked through sun an' rain, early in de mornin', and late at night; habn't I saved you an oberseer by doin' his work; hab you anyting to complain of agin me?"

"No, Joe; 'I've no complaint to make of you; you're a good nigger, and you've always worked well; but the first lesson my niggers have to learn is that I am *master*, and that they are not to resist or refuse to obey anything I tell 'em to do. So the first thing they've got to do, is to be whipped; if they resist, they got it all the harder; and so I'll go on, till I kill 'em, but they've got to give up at last, and learn that I'm master."

Joe thought it best to submit. He stripped off his upper clothing, and took his whipping, without a word; but as he drew his clothes up over his torn and bleeding back, he said, "Dis is de last!" That night he took a boat and went a long distance to the cabin of Harriet's father, and said, "Next time Moses comes, let me know." It was only a week or two after that, that the mysterious woman whom no one could lay their finger on appeared, and men, women, and children began to disappear from the plantations. One fine morning Joe was missing, and his brother William, from another plantation; Peter and Eliza, too, were gone; and these made part of Harriet's next party, who began their pilgrimage from Maryland to Canada, or as they expressed it, from "Egypt to de land of Canaan."

Their adventures were enough to fill a volume; they were pursued; they were hidden in "potato holes," while their pursuers passed within a few feet of them; they were passed along by friends in various disguises; they scattered and separated, to be led by guides by a roundabout way, to a meeting-place again. They were taken in by Sam Green, the man who was afterwards sent to State Prison for ten years for having a copy of "Uncle Tom's Cabin" in his house; and so, hunted and hiding and wandering, they came at last to the long bridge at the entrance of the city of Wilmington, Delaware. The rewards posted up everywhere had been at first five hundred dollars for Joe, if taken within the limits of the United States; then a thousand, and then fifteen hundred dollars, "an' all expenses clar an' clean, for his body in Easton Jail," Eight hundred for William, and four hundred for Peter, and twelve thousand for the woman who enticed them away. The long Wilmington Bridge was guarded by police officers, and the advertisements were everywhere. The party were scattered, and taken to the houses of different colored friends, and word was sent secretly to Thomas Garrett, of Wilmington, of their condition, and the necessity of their being taken across the bridge. Thomas Garrett is a Quaker, and a man of a wonderfully large and generous heart, through whose hands, Harriet tells me, two thousand self-emancipated slaves passed on their way to freedom. He was always ready, heart and hand and means, in aiding these poor fugitives, and rendered most efficient help to Harriet on many of her journeys back and forth. A letter received a few days since by the writer, from this noble-hearted philanthropist, will be given presently.

As soon as Thomas Garrett heard of the condition of these poor people, his plan was formed. He engaged two wagons, filled them with bricklayers, whom of course he paid well for their share in the enterprise, and sent them across the bridge. They went as if on a frolic, singing and shouting. The guards saw them pass, and of course expected them to re-cross the bridge. After nightfall (and fortunately it was a dark night) the same wagons went back, but with an addition to their party. The fugitives were on the bottom of the wagons, the bricklayers on the seats, still singing and shouting; and so they passed by the guards, who were entirely unsuspicious of the nature of the load the wagons contained, or of the amount of property thus escaping their hands. And so they made their way to New York. When they entered the anti-slavery office there, Joe was recognized at once by the description in the advertisement. "Well," said Mr. Oliver Johnson, "I am glad to see the man whose head is worth fifteen hundred dollars." At this Joe's heart sank. If the advertisement had got to New York, that place which it had taken them so many days and nights to reach, he thought he was in danger still. "And how far is it now to Canada?" he asked. When told how many miles, for they were to come through

New York State, and cross the Suspension Bridge, he was ready to give up. "From dat time Joe was silent," said Harriet; "he sang no more, he talked no more; he sat wid his head on his hand, and nobody could 'muse him or make him take any interest in anyting." They passed along in safety, and at length found themselves in the cars, approaching Suspension Bridge. The rest were very joyous and happy, but Joe sat silent and sad. Their fellow-passengers all seemed interested in and for them, and listened with tears, as Harriet and all their party lifted up their voices and sang:

> I'm on my way to Canada,
> That cold and dreary land;
> The sad effects of slavery,
> I can't no longer stand.
> I've served my master all my days,
> Widout a dime's reward;
> And now I'm forced to run away,
> To flee the lash abroad.
> Farewell, ole master, don't think hard of me,
> I'll travel on to Canada, where all the slaves are free.
>
>
> The hounds are baying on my track,
> Ole master comes behind.
> Resolved that he will bring me back,
> Before I cross de line;
> I'm now embarked for yonder shore,
> There a man's a man by law;
> The iron horse will bear me o'er,
> To shake de lion's paw.
> Oh, righteous Father, wilt thou not pity me,
> And aid me on to Canada where all the slaves are free.
>
>
> Oh, I heard Queen Victoria say,
> That if we would forsake
> Our native land of slavery,
> And come across the lake;
> That she was standin' on de shore,
> Wid arms extended wide,
> To give us all a peaceful home
> Beyond de rolling tide.
> Farewell, ole master, etc.

The cars began to cross the bridge. Harriet was very anxious to have her companions see the Falls. William, Peter, and Eliza came eagerly to look at the wonderful sight; but Joe sat still, with his head upon his hand.

"Joe, come look at de Falls! Joe, you fool you, come see de Falls! its your last chance." But Joe sat still and never raised his head. At length Harriet knew by the rise in the center of the bridge, and the descent on the other side, that they had crossed "the line." She sprang across to Joe's seat, shook him with all her might, and shouted, "Joe, you've shook de lion's paw!" Joe did not know what she meant. "Joe, you're *free!*" shouted Harriet. Then Joe's head went up, he raised his hands on high, and his face, streaming with tears, to heaven, and broke out in loud and thrilling tones:

>"Glory to God and Jesus too,
One more soul is safe!
Oh, go and carry de news,
One more soul got safe."

"Joe, come and look at de Falls!" called Harriet.

>"Glory to God and Jesus too,
One more soul got safe."
was all the answer. The cars stopped on the other side. Joe's feet were the first to
touch British soil, after those of the conductor.

Loud roared the waters of Niagara, but louder still ascended the anthem of praise from the
overflowing heart of the freeman. And can we doubt that the strain was taken up by angel
voices, and that through the arches of Heaven echoed and reechoed the strain:

>Glory to God in the Highest,
Glory to God and Jesus too,
One more soul is safe.

"The ladies and gentlemen gathered round him," said Harriet, "till I couldn't see Joe for the
crowd, only I heard 'Glory to God and Jesus too!' louder than ever." William went after him,
and pulled him, saying, "Joe, stop your noise! you act like a fool!" Then Peter ran it, and jerked
him mos' off his feet,–"Joe, stop your hollerin'! Folks 'll think you're crazy!" But Joe gave no
heed. The ladies were crying, and the tears like rain ran down Joe's sable cheeks. A lady reached
over her fine cambric handkerchief to him. Joe wiped his face, and then he spoke.

"Oh! if I'd felt like dis down South, it would hab taken *nine* men to take me; only one more
journey for me now, and dat is to Hebben!" "Well, you ole fool you," said Harriet, with whom
there seems but one step from the sublime to the ridiculous, "you might a' looked at de Falls
fust, and den gone to Hebben afterwards." She has seen Joe several times since, a happy and
industrious freeman in Canada.

When asked, as she often is, how it was possible that she was not afraid to go back, with
that tremendous price upon her head, Harriet always answers, "Why, don't I tell you, Missus,
t'wan't *me*, 'twas *de Lord!* I always *tole* him, 'I trust to you. I don't know where to go or what to
do, but I expect you to lead me,' an' he always did." At one time she was going down, watched
for everywhere, after there had been a meeting of slaveholders in the court-house of one of
the large cities of Maryland, and an added reward had been put upon her head, with various
threats of the different cruel devices by which she should be tortured and put to death; friends
gathered round her, imploring her not to go on directly in the face of danger and death, and
this was Harriet's answer to them:

"Now look yer! John saw the city, didn't he? Yes, John saw the city. Well, what did he see?
He saw twelve gates--three of dose gates was on de north--three of 'em was on de east--and
three of 'em was on de west –but dere was three of 'em on de *South* too; an' I reckon if dey kill
me down dere, I'll git into one of dem gates, don't you?"

Whether Harriet's ideas of the geographical bearings of the gates of the Celestial City, as
seen in the Apocalyptic vision, were correct or not, we cannot doubt that she was right in the
deduction her faith drew from them; and that *somewhere,* whether north, south, east, or west,
to our dim vision, there is a gate to be opened for Harriet, where the welcome will be given,
"Come in thou blessed of my Father."

Many of the stories told me by Harriet, in answer to questions, have been corroborated by
letters, some of which will appear in this book. Of others, I have not been able to procure
confirmation, owing to ignorance of the address of those conversant with the facts. I find among
her papers, many of which are defaced by being carried about with her for years, portions of

letters addressed to myself, by persons at the South, and speaking of the valuable assistance Harriet was rendering our soldiers in the hospital, and our armies in the field. At this time her manner of life, as related by herself, was this:

"Well, Missus, I'd go to de hospital, I would, early eb'ry mornin'. I'd get a big chunk of ice, I would, and put it in a basin, and fill it with water; den I'd take a sponge and begin. Fust man I'd come to, I'd thrash away de flies, an' dey'd rise, dey would, like bees roun' a hive. Den I'd begin to bathe der wounds, an' by de time I'd bathed off three or four, de fire and heat would have melted de ice and made de water warm, an' it would be as red as clar blood. Den I'd go an' git more ice, I would, an' by de time I got to de nex' ones, de flies would be roun' de fust ones, black an' thick as eber." In this way she worked, day after day, till late at night; then she went home to her little cabin, and made about fifty pies, a great quantity of ginger-bread, and two casks of root beer. These she would hire some contraband to sell for her through the camps, and thus she would provide her support for another day; for this woman never received pay or pension, and never drew for herself but twenty days' rations during the four years of her labors. At one time she was called away from Hilton Head, by one of our officers, to come to Fernandina, where the men were "dying off like sheep," from dysentery. Harriet had acquired quite a reputation for her skill in curing this disease, by a medicine which she prepared from roots which grew near the waters which gave the disease. Here she found thousands of sick soldiers and contrabands, and immediately gave up her time and attention to them. At another time, we find her nursing those who were down by hundreds with small-pox and malignant fevers. She had never had these diseases, but she seems to have no more fear of death in one form than another. "De Lord would take keer of her till her time came, an' den she was ready to go."

When our armies and gun-boats first appeared in any part of the South, many of the poor negroes were as much afraid of "de Yankee Buckra" as of their own masters. It was almost impossible to win their confidence, or to get information from them. But to Harriet they would tell anything; and so it became quite important that she should accompany expeditions going up the rivers, or into unexplored parts of the country, to control and get information from those whom they took with them as guides.

Gen. Hunter asked her at one time if she would go with several gunboats up the Combahee River, the object of the expedition being to take up the torpedoes placed by the rebels in the river, to destroy railroads and bridges, and to cut off supplies from the rebel troops. She said she would go if Col. Montgomery was to be appointed commander of the expedition. Col. Montgomery was one of John Brown's men, and was well known to Harriet. Accordingly, Col. Montgomery was appointed to the command, and Harriet, with several men under her, the principal of whom was J. Plowden, whose pass I have, accompanied the expedition. Harriet describes in the most graphic manner the appearance of the plantations as they passed up the river; the frightened negroes leaving their work and taking to the woods, at sight of the gun-boats; then coming to peer out like startled deer, and scudding away like the wind at the sound of the steam-whistle. "Well," said one old negro, "Mas'r said de Yankees had horns and tails, but I nebber beliebed it till now." But the word was passed along by the mysterious telegraphic communication existing among these simple people, that these were "Lincoln's gun-boats come to set them free." In vain, then, the drivers used their whips, in their efforts to hurry the poor creatures back to their quarters; they all turned and ran for the gun-boats. They came down every road, across every field, just as they had left their work and their cabins; women with children clinging around their necks, hanging to their dresses, running behind, all making at full speed for "Lincoln's gun-boats." Eight hundred poor wretches at one time crowded the banks, with their hands extended towards their deliverers, and they were all taken off upon the gunboats, and carried down to Beaufort.

"I nebber see such a sight," said Harriet; we laughed, an' laughed, an' laughed. Here you'd see a woman wid a pail on her head, rice a smokin' in it jus as she'd taken it from de fire, young one hangin' on behind, one han' roun' her forehead to hold on, 'tother han' diggin' into de rice-pot, eatin' wid all its might; hold of her dress two or three more; down her back a bag wid a pig in it. One woman brought two pigs, a white one, an' a black one; we took 'em all on board; named de white pig Beauregard, an' de black pig Jeff Davis. Sometimes de women would come wid twins hangin' roun' der necks; 'pears like I nebber see so many twins in my life; bags on der shoulders, baskets on der heads, and young ones taggin' behin', all loaded; pigs squealin', chickens screamin', young ones squallin'." And so they came pouring down to the gunboats. When they stood on the shore, and the small boats put out to take them off, they all wanted to get in at once. After the boats were crowded, they would hold on to them so that they could not leave the shore. The oarsmen would beat them on their hands, but they would not let go; they were afraid the gun-boats would go off and leave them, and all wanted to make sure of one of these arks of refuge. At length Col. Montgomery shouted from the upper deck, above the clamor of appealing tones, "Moses, you'll have to give 'em a song." Then Harriet lifted up her voice and sang:

"Of all the whole creation in the east or in the west,
The glorious Yankee nation is the greatest and the best.
Come along! Come along! don't be alarmed,
Uncle Sam is rich enough to give you all a farm."

At the end of every verse, the negroes in their enthusiasm would throw up their hands and shout "Glory," and the row-boats would take that opportunity to push off; and so at last they were all brought on board. The masters fled; houses and barns and railroad bridges were burned, tracks torn up, torpedoes destroyed, and the expedition was in all respects successful.

This fearless woman was often sent into the rebel lines as a spy, and brought back valuable information as to the position of armies and batteries; she has been in battle when the shot was falling like hail, and the bodies of dead and wounded men were dropping around her like leaves in autumn; but the thought of fear never seems to have had place for a moment in her mind. She had her duty to perform, and she expected to be taken care of till it was done.

Would that instead of taking them in this poor way at second-hand, my readers could hear this woman's graphic accounts of scenes she herself witnessed, could listen to her imitations of negro preachers in their own very peculiar dialect, her singing of camp-meeting hymns, her account of "experience meetings," her imitations of the dances, and the funeral ceremonies of these simple people. "Why, der language down dar in de far South is jus' as different from ours in Maryland, as you can think," said she. "Dey laughed when dey heard me talk, an' I could not understand dem, no how." She described a midnight funeral which she attended; for the slaves, never having been allowed to bury their dead in the day time, continued the custom of night funerals from habit.

The corpse was laid upon the ground, and the people all sat round, the group being lighted up by pine torches.

The old negro preacher began by giving out a hymn, which was sung by all. "An' oh! I wish you could hear 'em sing, Missus," said Harriet. "Der voices is so sweet, and dey can sing eberyting we sing, an' den dey can sing a great many hymns dat we can't nebber catch at all."

The old preacher began his sermon by pointing to the dead man, who lay in a rude box on the ground before him.

"Shum? Ded-a-de-dah! Shum, David? Ded-a-de-dah! Now I want you all to flec' for moment. Who ob all dis congregation is gwine next to lie ded-a-de-dah? You can't go nowheres, my frien's and bredren, but Deff 'll fin' you. You can't dig no hole so deep an' bury yourself dar, but God A'mighty's far-seein' eye 'll fine you, an' Deff 'll come arter you. You can't go into that big fort (pointing to Hilton Head), an' shut yourself up dar; dat fort dat Sesh Buckner said de debil couldn't take, but Deff 'll fin' you dar. All your frien's may forget you, but Deff 'll nebber forget you. Now, my bredren, prepare to lie ded-a-de-dah!"

This was the burden of a very long sermon, after which the whole congregation went round in a sort of solemn dance, called the "spiritual shuffle," shaking hands with each other, and calling each other by name as they sang:

My sis'r Mary's boun' to go;
My sis'r Nanny's boun' to go;
My brudder Tony's boun' to go;
My brudder July's boun' to go.

This to the same tune, till every hand had been shaken by every one of the company. When they came to Harriet, who was a stranger, they sang:

Eberybody's boun' to go!
The body was then placed in a Government wagon, and by the light of the pine torches, the strange, dark procession moved along, singing a rude funeral hymn, till they reached the place of burial.

Harriet's account of her interview with an old negro she met at Hilton Head, is amusing and interesting. He said "I'd been yere seventy-three years, workin' for my master widout even a dime wages. I'd worked rain-wet sun dry. I'd worked wid my mouf full of dust, but would not stop to get a drink of water. I'd been whipped, an' starved, an' I was always prayin', 'Oh! Lord, come an' delibber us!' All dat time de birds had been flyin', an' de rabens had been cryin', and de fish had been sunnin' in de waters. One day I look up, an' I see a big cloud; it didn't come up like as de clouds come out far yonder, but it 'peared to be right ober head. Der was tunders out of dat, an' der was lightnin's. Den I looked down on de water, an' I see, 'peared to me a big house in de water, an' out of de big house came great big eggs, and de good eggs went on trou' de air, an' fell into de fort; an' de bad eggs burst before dey got dar. Den de Sesh Buckra begin to run, an de neber stop running till de git to de swamp, an' de stick dar an' de die dar. Den I heard 'twas the Yankee ship[1] firin' out de big eggs, an dey had come to set us free. Den I praise de Lord. He come an' put he little finger in de work, an' dey Sesh Buckra all go; and de birds stop flyin', and de rabens stop cryin', an' when I go to catch a fish to eat wid my rice, de 's no fish dar. De Lord A'mighty 'd come and frightened 'em all out of de waters. Oh! Praise de Lord! I 'd prayed seventy-three years, an' now he 's come an' we's all free."

The last time Harriet was returning from the war, with her pass as hospital nurse, she bought a half-fare ticket, as she was told she must do; and missing the other train, she got into an emigrant train on the Amboy Railroad. When the conductor looked at her ticket, he said, "Come, hustle out of here! We don't carry niggers for half-fare." Harriet explained to him that she was in the employ of Government, and was entitled to transportation as the soldiers were. But the conductor took her forcibly by the arm, and said, "I'll make you tired of trying to stay here." She resisted, and being very strong, she could probably have got the better of the conductor, had he not called three men to his assistance. The car was filled with emigrants, and no one seemed to take her part. The only word, she heard, accompanied with fearful oaths, were, "Pitch the nagur out!" They nearly wrenched her arm off, and at length threw her, with all their strength, into a baggage-car. She supposed her arm was broken, and in intense suffering she came on to New York. As she left the car, a delicate-looking young man came up to her, and, handing her a card, said, "You ought to sue that conductor, and if you want a witness, call on me." Harriet remained all winter under the care of a physician in New York; he advised her to sue the Railroad company, and said that he would willingly testify as to her injuries. But the card the young man had given her was only a visiting card, and she did not know where to find him, and so she let the matter go.

The writer here finds it necessary to apologize for the very desultory and hasty manner in which this little book is written. Being herself pressed for time, in the expectation of soon leaving the country, she is obliged to pen down the material to be used in the short and interrupted interviews she can obtain with Harriet, and also to use such letters and accounts as may be sent her, as they come, without being able to work them in, in the order of time. A very material assistance is to be rendered her by the kind offer of an account of Harriet's services during the war, written by Mr. Charles P. Wood, of Auburn, and kindly copied by one of Harriet's most faithful and most efficient friends, Mrs. S. M. Hopkins, of that place.

It was a wise plan of our sagacious heroine to leave her old parents till the last to be brought away. They were pensioned off as too old to work, had a cabin, and a horse and cow, and were quite comfortable. If Harriet had taken them away before the young people, these last would have been sold into Southern slavery, to keep them out of her way. But at length Harriet heard that the old man had been betrayed by a slave whom he had assisted, but who had turned back, and when questioned by his wife, told her the story of his intended escape, and of the aid he had received from "Old Ben." This woman, hoping to curry favor with her master, revealed the whole to him, and "Old Ben" was arrested. He was to be tried the next week, when Harriet appeared upon the scene and, as she says, "saved dem de expense ob de trial," and removed her father to a higher court, by taking him off to Canada. The manner of their escape is detailed in the following letter from Thomas Garrett, the Wilmington Quaker:

WILMINGTON, 6th Mo., 1868.

MY FRIEND: Thy favor of the 12th reached me yesterday, requesting such reminiscences as I could give respecting the remarkable labors of Harriet Tubman, in aiding her colored friends from bondage. I may begin by saying, living as I have in a slave State, and the laws being very severe where my proof could be made of any one aiding slaves on their way to freedom, I have not felt at liberty to keep any written word of Harriet's or my own labors, except in numbering those whom I have aided. For that reason I cannot furnish so interesting an account of Harriet's labors as I otherwise could, and now would be glad to do; for in truth I never met with any person, of any color, who had more confidence in the voice of God, as spoken direct to her soul. She has frequently told me that she talked with God, and he talked with her every day of her life, and she has declared to me that she felt no more fear of being arrested by her former master, or any other person, when in his immediate neighborhood, than she did in the State of New York, or Canada, for she said she never ventured only where God sent her, and her faith in a Supreme Power truly was great.

I have now been confined to my room with indisposition more than four weeks, and cannot sit to write much; but I feel so much interested in Harriet that I will try to give some of the most remarkable incidents that now present themselves to my mind. The date of the commencement of her labors, I cannot certainly give; but I think it must have been about 1845; from that time till 1860, I think she must have brought from the neighborhood where she had been held as a slave, from 60 to 80 persons, from Maryland, some 80 miles from here. No slave who placed himself under her care, was ever arrested that I have heard of; she mostly had her regular stopping places on her route; but in one instance, when she had two stout men with her, some 30 miles below here, she said that God told her to stop, which she did; and then asked him what she must do. He told her to leave the road, and turn to the left; she obeyed, and soon came to a small stream of tide water; there was no boat, no bridge; she again inquired of her Guide what she was to do. She was told to go through. It was cold, in the month of March; but having confidence in her Guide, she went in; the water came up to her arm-pits; the men refused to follow till they saw her safe on the opposite shore. They then followed, and if I mistake not, she had soon to wade a second stream; soon after which she came to a cabin of colored people, who took them all in, put them to bed, and dried their clothes, ready to proceed next night on their journey. Harriet had run out of money, and gave them some of her underclothing to pay for their kindness. When she called on me two days after, she was so hoarse she could hardly speak, and was also suffering with violent toothache. The strange part of the story we found to be, that the master of these two men had put up the previous day, at the railroad station near where she left, an advertisement for them, offering a large reward for their apprehension; but they made a safe exit. She at one time brought as many as seven or eight, several of whom were women and children. She was well known here in Chester County and Philadelphia, and respected by all true abolitionists. I had been in the habit of furnishing her and those that accompanied her, as she returned from her acts of mercy, with new shoes; and on one occasion when I had not seen her for three months, she came into my store. I said, "Harriet, I am glad to see thee! I suppose thee wants a pair of new shoes." Her reply was "I want more than that." I, in jest, said, "I have always been liberal with thee, and wish to be; but I am not rich, and cannot afford to give much." Her reply was: "God tells me you have money for me." I asked her "if God never deceived her?" She said, "No!" "Well! how much does thee want?" After studying a moment, she said: "About twenty-three dollars." I then gave her twenty-four dollars and some odd cents, the net proceeds of five pounds sterling, received through Eliza Wigham, of Scotland, for her. I had given some accounts of Harriet's labor to the Anti-Slavery Society of Edinburgh, of which Eliza Wigham was Secretary. On the reading of my letter, a gentleman present said he would send Harriet four pounds if he knew of any way to get it to her. Eliza Wigham offered to forward it to me for her, and that was the first money ever received by me for her. Some twelve months after, she called on me again, and said that God told her I had some money for her, but not so much as before. I had, a few days previous, received the net proceeds of one pound ten shillings from Europe for her. To say the least, there was something remarkable in these facts, whether clairvoyance, or the divine impression on her mind from the source of all power, I cannot tell; but certain it was she had a guide within herself other than the written word, for she never had any education. She brought away her aged parents in a singular manner. They started with an old horse, fitted out in primitive style with a *straw collar,* a pair of old chaise wheels, with a board on the axle to sit on, another board swung with ropes, fastened to the axle, to rest their feet on. She got her parents, who were both slaves belonging to different masters, on this rude vehicle to the railroad, put them in the cars, turned Jehu herself, and drove to town in a style that no human being ever did before or since; but she was happy at having arrived safe. Next day, I furnished her with money to take them all to Canada. I afterwards sold their horse, and sent them the balance of the proceeds. I believe that Harriet succeeded in freeing all her relatives but one sister and her three children. Etc., etc.

Thy friend,

THOS. GARRETT.

Friend Garrett probably refers here to those who passed through his hands. Harriet was obliged to come by many different routes on her different journeys, and though she never counted those whom she brought away with her, it would seem, by the computation of others, that there must have been somewhere near three hundred brought by her to the Northern States and Canada.

Extracts from a letter written by Mr. Sanborn, Secretary of the Massachusetts Board of State Charities

My DEAR MADAME: Mr. Phillips has sent me your note, asking for reminiscences of Harriet Tubman, and testimonials to her extraordinary story, which all her New England friends will, I am sure, be glad to furnish.

I never had reason to doubt the truth of what Harriet said in regard to her own career, for I found her singularly truthful. Her imagination is warm and rich, and there is a whole region of the marvelous in her nature, which has manifested itself at times remarkably. Her dreams and visions, misgivings and forewarnings, ought not to be omitted in any life of her, particularly those relating to John Brown.

She was in his confidence in 1858-9, and he had a great regard for her, which he often expressed to me. She aided him in his plans, and expected to do so still further, when his career was closed by that wonderful campaign in Virginia. The first time she came to my house, in Concord, after that tragedy, she was shown into a room in the evening, where Brackett's bust of John Brown was standing. The sight of it, which was new to her, threw her into a sort of ecstacy of sorrow and admiration, and she went on in her rhapsodical way to pronounce his apotheosis.

She has often been in Concord, where she resided at the houses of Emerson, Alcott, the Whitneys, the Brooks family, Mrs. Horace Mann, and other well known persons. They all admired and respected her, and nobody doubted the reality of her adventures. She was too *real* a person to be suspected. In 1862, I think it was, she went from Boston to Port Royal, under the advice and encouragement of Mr. Garrison, Governor Andrew, Dr. Howe, and other leading people. Her career in South Carolina is well known to some of our officers, and I think to Colonel Higginson, now of Newport, R. I., and Colonel James Montgomery, of Kansas, to both of whom she was useful as a spy and guide, if I mistake not. I regard her as, on the whole, the most extraordinary person of her race I have ever met. She is a negro of pure or almost pure blood, can neither read nor write, and has the characteristics of her race and condition. But she has done what can scarcely be credited on the best authority, and she has accomplished her purposes with a coolness, foresight, patience, and wisdom, which in a *white man* would have raised him to the highest pitch of reputation.

I am, dear Madame, very truly your servant,

F. B. SANBORN.

Of the "dreams and visions" mentioned in this letter, the writer might have given many wonderful instances; but it was thought best not to insert anything which, with any, might bring discredit upon the story. When these turns of somnolency come upon Harriet, she imagines that her "spirit" leaves her body, and visits other scenes and places, not only in this world, but in the world of spirits. And her ideas of these scenes show, to say the least of it, a vividness of imagination seldom equaled in the soarings of the most cultivated minds.

Not long since, the writer, on going into Harriet's room in the morning, sat down by her and began to read that wonderful and glorious description of the heavenly Jerusalem in the two last chapters of Revelations. When the reading was finished, Harriet burst into a rhapsody which perfectly amazed her hearer--telling of what she had seen in one of these visions, sights which no one could doubt had been real to her, and which no human imagination could have conceived, it would seem, unless in dream or vision. There was a wild poetry in these descriptions which seemed to border almost on inspiration, but by many they might be characterized as the ravings of insanity. All that can be said is, however, if this woman is insane, there has been a wonderful "method in her madness."

At one time, Harriet was much troubled in spirit about her three brothers, feeling sure that some great evil was impending over their heads. She wrote a letter, by the hand of a friend, to a man named Jacob Jackson, who lived near there. Jacob was a free negro, who could both read and write, and who was under suspicion at that time, as it was thought he had something to do with the disappearance of so many slaves. It was necessary, therefore, to be very cautious in writing to him. Jacob had an adopted son, William Henry Jackson, also free, who had come South; and so Harriet determined to sign her letter with his name, knowing that Jacob would be clever enough to understand, by her peculiar phraseology, what meaning she intended to convey to him. She, therefore, after speaking of indifferent matters, said, "Read my letter to the old folks, and give my love to them, and tell my brothers to be always *watching unto prayer,* and when the *good old ship of Zion comes along, to be ready to step aboard."*

The letter was signed "William Henry Jackson." Jacob was not allowed to have his letters till the self-elected inspectors had had the reading of them, and studied into their secret meaning. They, therefore, got together, wiped their glasses, and got them on, and proceeded to a careful perusal of this mysterious document. What it meant, they could not imagine; William Henry Jackson had no parents or brothers, and the letter was incomprehensible. White genius having exhausted itself, black genius was called in, and Jacob's letter was at last handed to him. Jacob saw at once what it meant, but tossed it down, saying, "Dat letter can't be meant for me, no how. I can't make head nor tail of it," and walked off and took immediate measures to let Harriet's brothers know secretly that she was coming, and they must be ready to start at a moment's notice for the North. When Harriet arrived there, it was the day before Christmas, and she found her three brothers, who had attempted to escape, were advertised to be sold on Christmas day to the highest bidder, to go down to the cotton and rice fields with the chain gang. Christmas came on Sunday, and therefore they were not to be sold till Monday. Harriet arrived on Saturday, and gave them secret notice to be ready to start Saturday night, immediately after dark, the first stopping-place to be their father's cabin, forty miles away. When they assembled, their brother John was missing; but when Harriet was ready, the word was "Forward!" and she "nebber waited for no one." Poor John was almost ready to start, when his wife was taken ill, and in an hour or two, another little inheritor of the blessings of slavery had come into the world. John must go off for a "Granny," and then he would not leave his wife in her present circumstances. But after the birth of the child, he began to think he must start; the North and Liberty, or the South and life-long Slavery--these were the alternatives, and this was his last chance. He tried again and again to steal out of the door, but a watchful eye was on him, and he was always arrested by the question, "Where you gwine John?" At length he told her he was going to try to see if he couldn't get hired out on Christmas to another man. His wife did not think that he was to be sold. He went out of the door, and stood by the corner of the house, near her bed, listening. At length, he heard her sobbing and crying, and not being able to endure it, he went back. "Oh! John," said his wife, "you's gwine to lebe me; but, wherebber you go, remember me an' de chillen." John went out and started at full speed for his father's cabin, forty miles away. At daybreak, he overtook the others in the "fodder house," near the cabin of their parents. Harriet had not seen her mother there for six years, but they did not dare to let the old woman know of their being in her neighborhood, or of their intentions, for she would have raised such an uproar in her efforts to detain them with her, that the whole plantation would have been alarmed. The poor old woman had been expecting the boys all day, to spend Christmas with her as usual. She had been hard at work, had killed a pig, and put it to all the various uses to which sinner's flesh is doomed, and had made all the preparations her circumstances admitted of, to give them a sumptuous entertainment, and there she sat watching. In the night, when Harriet and two of her brothers and two other men, who had escaped with them, arrived at the "fodder house," they were exhausted and famished. They sent the two strange men up to the house to try and speak to "Old Ben," their father, but not to let their mother know of their being in the neighborhood. The men succeeded in rousing old Ben, who came out, and as soon as he heard their story, he gathered together a quantity of provisions, and came down to the fodder house, and slipped them inside the door, taking care not to *see* his children. Up among the ears of corn they lay, and one of them he had not seen for six years. It rained very hard all that Sunday, and there they lay all day, for they could not start till night. At about daybreak, John joined them. There were wide chinks in the boards of the fodder house, and through them they could see their father's cabin; and all day long, every few minutes, they would see the old woman come out, and, shading her eyes with her hand, take a long look down the road to see if her children were coming, and then they could almost hear her sigh as she turned into the house, disappointed.

Two or three times, the old man came down, and pushed food inside the door, and after nightfall he came to accompany them part of the way upon their journey. When he reached the fodder house, he tied his handkerchief tight over his eyes, and two of his sons taking him by each arm, he accompanied them some miles upon their journey. They then bade him farewell, and left him standing blind-fold in the middle of the road. When he could no longer hear their footsteps, he took off the handkerchief, and turned back.

But before leaving, they had gone up to the cabin to take a silent farewell of the poor old mother. Through the little window of the cabin, they saw the old woman sitting by her fire with a pipe in her mouth, her head on her hand, rocking back and forth as she did when she was in trouble, and wondering what new evil had come to her children. With streaming eyes, they watched her for ten or fifteen minutes; but time was precious, and they must reach their next station before daybreak, and so they turned sadly away.

When the holidays were over, and the men came for the three brothers to sell them, they could not be found. The first place to search was of course the plantation where all their relatives and friends lived. They went to the "big house," and asked the "Doctor" if he had seen anything of them. The Doctor said, "No, they mostly came up there to see the other niggers when they came for Christmas, but they hadn't been round at all." "Have you been down to Old Ben's?" the Doctor asked. "Yes." "What does Old Rit say?" "Old Rit says not one of 'em came this Christmas. She was looking for 'em most all day, and most broke her heart about it." "What does Old Ben say?" "Old Ben says that he hasn't seen one of his children this Christmas." "Well, if Old Ben says that, they haven't been round." And so the man-hunters went off disappointed.

One of the other brothers, William Henry, had long been attached to a girl named Catherine, who lived with another master; but her master would not let her marry him. When William Henry made up his mind to start with Harriet, he determined to bring Catherine with him. And so he went to a tailor's, and bought a new suit of men's clothes, and threw them over the garden fence of Catherine's master. The garden ran down to a run, and Catherine had been notified where to find the clothes. When the time had come to get ready, Catherine went to the foot of the garden and dressed herself in the suit of men's clothes. She was soon missed, and all the girls in the house were set to looking for Catherine. Presently they saw coming up through the garden, as if from the river, a well-dressed little darkey, and they all stopped looking for Catherine to stare at him. He walked directly by them round the house, and went out of the gate, without the slightest suspicion being excited as to who he was. In a fortnight from that time, the whole party were safe in Canada.

William Henry died in Canada, but Catherine has been seen and talked with by the writer, at the house of the old people.

Of the many letters, testimonials, and passes, placed in the hands of the writer by Harriet, the following are selected for insertion in this book, and are quite sufficient to verify her statements.

A Letter from Gen. Saxton to a Lady of Auburn.

ATLANTA, GA., March 21, 1868.

MY DEAR MADAME: I have just received your letter informing me that Hon. Wm. H. Seward, Secretary of State, would present a petition to Congress for a pension to Harriet Tubman, for services rendered in the Union Army during the late war. I can bear witness to the value of her services in South Carolina and Florida. She was employed in the hospitals and as a spy. She made many a raid inside the enemy's lines, displaying remarkable courage, zeal, and fidelity. She was employed by General Hunter, and I think by Generals Stevens and Sherman, and is as deserving of a pension from the Government for her services as any other of its faithful servants.

I am very truly yours,

RUFUS SAXTON, Bvt. Brig.-Gen. U. S. A.

Letter from Hon. Wm. H. Seward.

WASHINGTON, July 25,1868.

MAJ.-GEN. HUNTER--

My DEAR SIR: Harriet Tubman, a colored woman, has been nursing our soldiers during nearly all the war. She believes she has a claim for faithful services to the command in South Carolina with which you are connected, and she thinks that you would be disposed to see her claim justly settled.

I have known her long, and a nobler, higher spirit, or a truer, seldom dwells in the human form. I commend her, therefore, to your kind and best attentions.

Faithfully your friend,
WILLIAM H. SEWARD.

Letter from Col. James Montgomery.

ST. HELENA ISLAND, S. C., July 6, 1863.
HEADQUARTERS COLORED BRIGADE.

BRIG.-GEN. GILMAN, Commanding Department of the South--

GENERAL: I wish to commend to your attention, Mrs. Harriet Tubman, a most remarkable woman, and invaluable as a scout. I have been acquainted with her character and actions for several years.

Walter D. Plowden is a man of tried courage, and can be made highly useful.

I am, General, your most ob't servant,

JAMES MONTGOMERY, Col. Com. Brigade.

Letter from Mrs. Gen. A. Baird.

PETERBORO, Nov. 24,1864.

The bearer of this, Harriet Tubman, a most excellent woman, who has rendered faithful and good services to our Union army, not only in the hospital, but in various capacities, having been employed under Government at Hilton Head, and in Florida; and I commend her to the protection of all officers in whose department she may happen to be.

She has been known and esteemed for years by the family of my uncle, Hon. Gerrit Smith, as a person of great rectitude and capabilities.

Mrs. GEN. A. BAIRD.

Letter from Hon. Gerrit Smith.

PETERBORO, N. Y., Nov. 4,1867.

I have known Mrs. Harriet Tubman for many years. Seldom, if ever, have I met with a person more philanthropic, more self-denying, and of more bravery. Nor must I omit to say that she combines with her sublime spirit, remarkable discernment and judgment.

During the late war, Mrs. Tubman was eminently faithful and useful to the cause of our country. She is poor and has poor parents. Such a servant of the country should be well paid by the country. I hope that the Government will look into her case.

GERRIT SMITH.

Testimonial from Gerrit Smith.

PETERBORO, Nov. 22,1864.

The bearer, Harriet Tubman, needs not any recommendation. Nearly all the nation over, she has been heard of for her wisdom, integrity, patriotism, and bravery. The cause of freedom owes her much. The country owes her much.

I have known Harriet for many years, and I hold her in my high esteem.

GERRIT SMITH.

Certificate from Henry K. Durrant, Acting Asst Surgeon, U. S. A.

I certify that I have been acquainted with Harriet Tubman for nearly two years; and my position as Medical Officer in charge of "contrabands" in this town and in hospital, has given me frequent and ample opportunities to observe her general deportment; particularly her kindness and attention to the sick and suffering of her own race. I take much pleasure in testifying to the esteem in which she is generally held.

HENRY K. DURRANT,
Acting Assistant Surgeon, U. S. A. In charge "Contraband" Hospital.

Dated at Beaufort, S. C., the 3d day of May, 1864. I concur fully in the above.
R. SAXTON, Brig.-Gen. Vol.

The following are a few of the passes used by Harriet throughout the war. Many others are so defaced that it is impossible to decipher them.

HEADQUARTERS DEPARTMENT OF THE SOUTH,
HILTON HEAD, PORT ROYAL, S. C., Feb. 19, 1863.

Pass the bearer, Harriet Tubman, to Beaufort and back to this place, and wherever she wishes to go; and give her free passage at all times, on all Government transports. Harriet was sent to me from Boston by Gov. Andrew of Mass., and is a valuable woman. She has permission, as a servant of the Government, to purchase such provisions from the Commissary as she may need.

D. HUNTER, Maj.-Gen. Com.

General Gillman, who succeeded General Hunter in command of the Department of the South, appends his signature to the same pass.

HEADQUARTERS OF THE DEPARTMENT OF THE SOUTH,
July 1, 1863.

Continued in force.

I. A. GILLMAN, Brig.-Gen. Com.

BEAUFORT, Aug. 28,1862.

Will Capt. Warfield please let "Moses" have a little Bourbon whiskey for medicinal purposes.

HENRY K. DURRANT, Act. Ass. Surgeon.

WAR DEPARTMENT, WASHINGTON, D. C.,
March 20,1865.

Pass Mrs. Harriet Tubman (colored) to Hilton Head and Charleston, S. C., with free transportation on a Government transport.
By order of the Sec. of War.

Louis H., Asst. Adj.-Gen., U. S. A.

To Bvt. Brig.-Gen. Van Vliet, U. S. Q. M., N. Y.

Not transferable.

WAR DEPARTMENT, WASHINGTON, D. C.,
July 22,1865.

Permit Harriet Tubman to proceed to Fortress Monroe, Va., on a Government transport. Transportation will be furnished free of cost.

By order of the Secretary of War.

L. H., Asst. Adj.-Gen.

Not transferable.

Appointment as Nurse.

SIR:–I have the honor to inform you that the Medical Director Department of Virginia has been instructed to appoint Harriet Tubman nurse or matron at the Colored Hospital, Fort Monroe, Va.

Very respectfully, your obdt. servant,

V. K. BARNES, Surgeon-General.

Hon. WM. H. SEWARD,

Secretary of State, Washington, D. C.

Names of Harriet's Assistants, Scouts, or Pilots.

Scouts who are residents of Beaufort, and well acquainted with the main land: Peter Barns, Mott Blake, Sandy Selters, Solomon Gregory, Isaac Hayward, Gabriel Cohen, George Chrisholm.

Pilots who know the channels of the rivers in this vicinity, and who acted as such for Col. Montgomery up the Combahee River: Charles Simmons, Samuel Hayward.

App'd, R. SAXTON, Brig.-Gen.

At this point the following good and kind letter from Rev. Henry Fowler is received:

AUBURN, June 23,1868.

MY DEAR FRIEND:–I wish to say to you how gratified I am that you are writing the biography of Harriet Tubman. I feel that her life forms part of the history of the country, and that it ought not to depend upon tradition to keep it in remembrance. Had not the pressure of professional claims prevented, I should have aspired to be her historian myself; but my disappointment in this regard is more than met by the satisfaction experienced in hearing that you are the chosen Miriam of this African "Moses;" the name by which she was known among her emancipated followers from the land of bondage. Blessed be God! a "Greater than Moses" has at last broken every bond.

As ever, with warm regard, your friend,

HENRY FOWLER.

The following account of the subject of this memoir is cut from the *Boston Commonwealth* of 1863, kindly sent the writer by Mr. Sanborn:

"It was said long ago that the true romance of America was not in the fortunes of the Indian, where Cooper sought it, nor in the New England character, where Judd found it, nor in the social contrasts of Virginia planters, as Thackeray imagined, but in the story of the fugitive slaves. The observation is as true now as it was before war, with swift, gigantic hand, sketched the vast shadows, and dashed in the high lights in which romance loves to lurk and flash forth. But the stage is enlarged on which those dramas are played, the whole world now sit as spectators, and the desperation or the magnanimity of a poor black woman has power to shake the nation that so long was deaf to her cries. We write of one of these heroines, of whom our slave annals are full,–a woman whose career is as extraordinary as the most famous of her sex can show.

"Araminta Ross, now known by her married name of Tubman, with her sounding Christian name changed to Harriet, is the grand-daughter of a slave imported from Africa, and has not a drop of white blood in her veins. Her parents were Benjamin Ross and Harriet Greene, both slaves, but married and faithful to each other. They still live in old age and poverty, but free, on a little property at Auburn, N. Y., which their daughter purchased for them from Mr. Seward, the Secretary of State. She was born, as near as she can remember, in 1820 or in 1821, in Dorchester County, on the Eastern shore of Maryland, and not far from the town of Cambridge. She had ten brothers and sisters, of whom three are now living, all at the North, and all rescued from slavery by Harriet, before the War. She went back just as the South was preparing to secede, to bring away a fourth, but before she could reach her, she was dead. Three years before, she had brought away her old father and mother, at great risk to herself.

"When Harriet was six years old, she was taken from her mother and carried ten miles to live with James Cook, whose wife was a weaver, to learn the trade of weaving. While still a mere child, Cook set her to watching his musk-rat traps, which compelled her to wade through the water. It happened that she was once sent when she was ill with the measles, and, taking cold from wading in the water in this condition, she grew very sick, and her mother persuaded her master to take her away from Cook's until she could get well.

"Another attempt was made to teach her weaving, but she would not learn, for she hated her mistress, and did not want to live at home, as she would have done as a weaver, for it was the custom then to weave the cloth for the family, or a part of it, in the house.

"Soon after she entered her teens she was hired out as a field hand, and it was while thus employed that she received a wound which nearly proved fatal, from the effects of which she still suffers. In the fall of the year, the slaves there work in the evening, cleaning up wheat, husking corn, etc. On this occasion, one of the slaves of a farmer named Barrett, left his work, and went to the village store in the evening. The overseer followed him, and so did Harriet. When the slave was found, the overseer swore he should be whipped, and called on Harriet, among others, to help tie him. She refused, and as the man ran away, she placed herself in the door to stop pursuit. The overseer caught up a two-pound weight from the counter and threw it at the fugitive, but it fell short and struck Harriet a stunning blow on the head. It was long before she recovered from this, and it has left her subject to a sort of stupor or lethargy at times; coming upon her in the midst of conversation, or whatever she may be doing, and throwing her into a deep slumber, from which she will presently rouse herself, and go on with her conversation or work.

"After this she lived for five or six years with John Stewart, where at first she worked in the house, but afterwards 'hired her time,' and Dr. Thompson, son of her master's guardian, 'stood for her,' that is, was her surety for the payment of what she owed. She employed the time thus hired in the rudest labors,—drove oxen, carted, plowed, and did all the work of a man,—sometimes earning money enough in a year, beyond what she paid her master, 'to buy a pair of steers,' worth forty dollars. The amount exacted of a woman for her time was fifty or sixty dollars,—of a man, one hundred to one hundred and fifty dollars. Frequently Harriet worked for her father, who was a timber inspector, and superintended the cutting and hauling of great quantities of timber for the Baltimore shipyards. Stewart, his temporary master, was a builder, and for the work of Ross used to receive as much as five dollars a day sometimes, he being a superior workman. While engaged with her father, she would cut wood, haul logs, etc. Her usual 'stint' was half a cord of wood in a day.

"Harriet was married somewhere about 1844, to a free colored man named John Tubman, but she had no children. For the last two years of slavery she lived with Dr. Thompson, before mentioned, her own master not being yet of age, and Dr. T.'s father being his guardian, as well as the owner of her own father. In 1849 the young man died, and the slaves were to be sold, though previously set free by an old will. Harriet resolved not to be sold, and so, with no knowledge of the North –having only heard of Pennsylvania and New Jersey--she walked away one night alone. She found a friend in a white lady, who knew her story and helped her on her way. After many adventures, she reached Philadelphia, where she found work and earned a small stock of money. With this money in her purse, she traveled back to Maryland for her husband, but she found him married to another woman, and no longer caring to live with her. This, however, was not until two years after her escape, for she does not seem to have reached her old home in her first two expeditions. In December, 1850, she had visited Baltimore and brought away her sister and two children, who had come up from Cambridge in a boat, under charge of her sister's husband, a free black. A few months after she had brought away her brother and two other men, but it was not till the fall of 1851 that she found her husband and learned of his infidelity. She did not give way to rage or grief, but collected a part of fugitives and brought them safely to Philadelphia. In December of the same year, she returned, and led out a party of eleven, among them her brother and his wife. With these she journeyed to Canada, and there spent the winter, for this was after the enforcement of Mason's Fugitive Slave Bill in Philadelphia and Boston, and there was no safety except 'under the paw of the British Lion,' as she quaintly said. But the first winter was terribly severe for these poor runaways. They earned their bread by chopping wood in the snows of a Canadian forest; they were frost-bitten, hungry, and naked. Harriet was their good angel. She kept house for her brother, and the poor creatures boarded with her. She worked for them, begged for them, prayed for them, with the strange familiarity of communion with God which seems natural to these people, and carried them by the help of God through the hard winter.

"In the spring she returned to the States, and as usual earned money by working in hotels and families as a cook. From Cape May, in the fall of 1852, she went back once more to Maryland, and brought away nine more fugitives.

"Up to this time she had expended chiefly her own money in these expeditions--money which she had earned by hard work in the drudgery of the kitchen. Never did any one more exactly fulfill the sense of George Herbert--

"A servant with this clause
Makes drudgery divine."

"But it was not possible for such virtues long to remain hidden from the keen eyes of the Abolitionists. She became known to Thomas Garrett, the large-hearted Quaker of Wilmington, who has aided the escape of three thousand fugitives; she found warm friends in Philadelphia and New York, and wherever she went. These gave her money, which she never spent for her own use, but laid up for the help of her people, and especially for her journeys back to the 'land of Egypt,' as she called her old home. By reason of her frequent visits there, always carrying away some of the oppressed, she got among her people the name of 'Moses,' which it seems she still retains.

"Between 1852 and 1857, she made but two of these journeys, in consequence partly of the increased vigilance of the slaveholders, who had suffered so much by the loss of their property. A great reward was offered for her capture, and she several times was on the point of being taken, but always escaped by her quick wit, or by 'warnings' from Heaven--for it is time to notice one singular trait in her character. She is the most shrewd and practical person in the world, yet she is a firm believer in omens, dreams, and warnings. She declares that before her escape from slavery, she used to dream of flying over fields and towns, and rivers and mountains, looking down upon them 'like a bird,' and reaching at last a great fence, or sometimes a river, over which she would try to fly, 'but it 'peard like I wouldn't hab de strength, and jes as I was sinkin' down, dare would be ladies all drest in white ober dere, and dey would put out dere arms and pull me 'cross.' There is nothing strange in this, perhaps, but she declares that when she came North she remembered these very places as those she had seen in her dreams, and many of the ladies who befriended her were those she had been helped by in her visions.

"Then she says she always knows when there is danger near her,--she does not know how, exactly, but ' 'pears like my heart go flutter, flutter, and den dey may say "Peace, Peace," as much as dey likes, *I know its gwine to be war!*' She is very firm on this point, and ascribes to this her great impunity, in spite of the lethargy before mentioned, which would seem likely to throw her into the hands of her enemies. She says she inherited this power, that her father could always predict the weather, and that he foretold the Mexican war.

"In 1857 she made her most venturesome journey, for she brought with her to the North her old parents, who were no longer able to walk such distances as she must go by night. Consequently she must hire a wagon for them, and it required all her ingenuity to get them through Maryland and Delaware safe. She accomplished it, however, and by the aid of her friends she brought them safe to Canada, where they spent the winter. Her account of their sufferings there--of her mother's complaining and her own philosophy about it--is a lesson of trust in Providence better than many sermons. But she decided to bring them to a more comfortable place, and so she negotiated with Mr. Seward--then in the Senate--for a little patch of ground with a house on it, at Auburn, near his own home. To the credit of the Secretary of State it should be said, that he sold her the property on very favorable terms, and gave her some time for payment. To this house she removed her parents, and set herself to work to pay for her purchase. It was on this errand that she first visited Boston--we believe in the winter of 1858-9. She brought a few letters from her friends in New York, but she could herself neither read nor write, and she was obliged to trust to her wits that they were delivered to the right persons. One of them, as it happened, was to the present writer, who received it by another hand, and called to see her at her boarding-house. It was curious to see the caution with which she received her visitor until she felt assured that there was no mistake. One of her means of security was to carry with her the daguerreotypes of her friends, and show them to each new person. If they recognized the likeness, then it was all right.

"Pains were taken to secure her the attention to which her great services to humanity entitled her, and she left New England with a handsome sum of money towards the payment of her debt to Mr. Seward. Before she left, however, she had several interviews with Captain Brown, then in Boston. He is supposed to have communicated his plans to her, and to have been aided by her in obtaining recruits and money among her people. At any rate, he always spoke of her with the greatest respect, and declared that 'General Tubman,' as he styled her, was a better officer than most whom he had seen, and could command an army as successfully as she had led her small parties of fugitives.

"Her own veneration for Captain Brown has always been profound, and since his murder, has taken the form of a religion. She had often risked her own life for her people, and she thought nothing of that; but that a white man, and a man so noble and strong, should so take upon himself the burden of a despised race, she could not understand, and she took refuge from her perplexity in the mysteries of her fervid religion.

"Again, she laid great stress on a dream which she had just before she met Captain Brown in Canada. She thought she was in 'a wilderness sort of place, all full of rocks and bushes,' when she saw a serpent raise its head among the rocks, and as it did so, it became the head of an old man with a long white beard, gazing at her 'wishful like, jes as ef he war gwine to speak to me,' and then two other heads rose up beside him, younger than he,– and as she stood looking at them, and wondering what they could want with her, a great crowd of men rushed in and struck down the younger heads, and then the head of the old man, still looking at her so 'wishful.' This dream she had again and again, and could not interpret it; but, when she met Captain Brown, shortly after, behold, he was the very image of the head she had seen. But still she could not make out what her dream signified, till the news came to her of the tragedy of Harper's Ferry, and then she knew the two other heads were his two sons. She was in New York at that time, and on the day of the affair at Harper's Ferry, she felt her usual warning that something was wrong--she could not tell what. Finally she told her hostess that it must be Captain Brown who was in trouble, and that they should soon hear bad news from him. The next day's newspaper brought tidings of what had happened.

"Her last visit to Maryland was made after this, in December, 1860; and in spite of the agitated condition of the country, and the greater watchfulness of the slaveholders, she brought away seven fugitives, one of them an infant, which must be drugged with opium to keep it from crying on the way, and so revealing the hiding place of the party. She brought these safely to New York, but there a new difficulty met her. It was the mad winter of compromises, when State after State, and politician after politician, went down on their knees to beg the South not to secede. The hunting of fugitive slaves began again. Mr. Seward went over to the side of compromise. He knew the history of this poor woman; he had given his enemies a hold on him, by dealing with her; it was thought he would not scruple to betray her. The suspicion was an unworthy one, for though the Secretary could betray a cause, he could not surely have put her enemies on the track of a woman who was thus in his power, after such a career as hers had been. But so little confidence was then felt in Mr. Seward, by men who had voted for him and with him, that they hurried Harriet off to Canada, sorely against her will.

"She did not long remain there. The war broke out, for which she had been long looking, and she hastened to her New England friends to prepare for another expedition to Maryland, to bring away the last of her family.

"Before she could start, however, the news came of the capture of Port Royal. Instantly she conceived the idea of going there and working among her people on the islands and the mainland. Money was given her, a pass was secured through the agency of Governor Andrew, and she went to Beaufort. There she has made herself useful in many ways--has been employed as a spy by General Hunter, and finally has piloted Col. Montgomery on his most successful expedition. We gave some notice of this fact last week. Since then we have received the following letter, dictated by her, from which it appears that she needs some contributions for her work. We trust she will receive them, for none has better deserved it. She asks nothing for herself, except that her wardrobe may be replenished, and even this she will probably share with the first needy person she meets.

" 'BEAUFORT, S. C., June 30, 1863.

* * * "'Last fall, when the people here became very much alarmed for fear of an invasion from the rebels, all my clothes were packed and sent with others to Hilton Head, and lost; and I have never been able to get any trace of them since. I was sick at the time, and unable to look after them myself. I want, among the rest, a *bloomer* dress, made of some coarse, strong material, to wear on *expeditions.* In our late expedition up the Combahee River, in coming on board the boat, I was carrying *two pigs* for a poor sick woman, who had a child to carry, and the order "double quick" was given, and I started to run, stepped on my dress, it being rather long, and fell and tore it almost off, so that when I got on board the boat, there was hardly anything left of it but shreds. I made up my mind then I would never wear a long dress on another expedition of the kind, but would have a *bloomer* as soon as I could get it. So please make this known to the ladies, if you will, for I expect to have use for it very soon, probably before they can get it to me.

"'You have, without doubt, seen a full account of the expedition I refer to. Don't you think we colored people are entitled to some credit for that exploit, under the lead of the brave Colonel Montgomery? We weakened the rebels somewhat on the Combahee River, by taking and bring-ing away *seven hundred and fifty-six* head of their most valuable live stock, known up in your re-gion as "contrabands," and this, too, without the loss of a single life on our part, though we had good reason to believe that a number of rebels bit the dust. Of these seven hundred and fifty-six contrabands, nearly or quite all the able-bodied men have joined the colored regiments here.

"'I have now been absent two years almost, and have just got letters from my friends in Auburn, urging me to come home. My father and mother are old and in feeble health, and need my care and attention. I hope the good people there will not allow them to suffer, and I do not believe they will. But I do not see how I am to leave at present the very important work to be done here. Among other duties which I have, is that of looking after the hospital here for contrabands. Most of those coming from the mainland are very destitute, almost naked. I am trying to find places for those able to work, and provide for them as best I can, so as to lighten the burden on the Government as much as possible, while at the same time they learn to respect themselves by earning their own living.

" 'Remember me very kindly to Mrs.–and her daughters; also, if you will, to my Boston friends, Mrs. C., Miss H., and especially to Mr. and Mrs. George L. Stearns, to whom I am under great obligations for their many kindnesses. I shall be sure to come and see you all if I live to go North. If you write, direct your letter to the care of C.'"

In the Spring of 1860, Harriet Tubman was requested by Mr. Gerrit Smith to go to Boston to attend a large Anti-Slavery meeting. On her way, she stopped at Troy to visit a cousin, and while there, the colored people were one day startled with the intelligence that a fugitive slave, by the name of Charles Nalle, had been followed by his master (who was his younger brother, and not one grain whiter than he), and that he was already in the hands of the officers, and was to be taken back to the South. The instant Harriet heard the news, she started for the office of the U. S. Commissioner, scattering the tidings as she went. An excited crowd were gathered about the office, through which Harriet forced her way, and rushed up stairs to the door of the room where the fugitive was detained. A wagon was already waiting before the door to carry off the man, but the crowd was even then so great, and in such a state of excitement, that the officers did not dare to bring the man down. On the opposite side of the street stood the colored people, watching the window where they could see Harriet's sun-bonnet, and feeling assured that so long as she stood there, the fugitive was still in the office. Time passed on, and he did not appear. "They've taken him out another way, depend upon that," said some of the colored people. "No," replied others, "there stands 'Moses' yet, and as long as she is there, he is safe." Harriet, now seeing the necessity for a tremendous effort for his rescue, sent out some little boys to cry *fire*. The bells rang, the crowd increased, till the whole street was a dense mass of people. Again and again the officers came out to try and clear the stairs, and make a way to take their captive down; others were driven down, but Harriet stood her ground, her head bent down, and her arms folded. "Come, old woman, you must get out of this," said one of the officers; "I must have the way cleared; if you can't get down alone, some one will help you." Harriet, still putting on a greater appearance of decrepitude, twitched away from him, and kept her place. Offers were made to buy Charles from his master, who at first agreed to take twelve hundred dollars for him; but when that was subscribed, he immediately raised the price to fifteen hundred. The crowd grew more excited. A gentleman raised a window and called out, "Two hundred dollars for his rescue, but not one cent to his master!" This was responded to by a roar of satisfaction from the crowd below. At length the officers appeared, and announced to the crowd that if they would open a lane to the wagon, they would promise to bring the man down the front way.

The lane was opened, and the man was brought out--a tall, handsome, intelligent *white* man, with his wrists manacled together, walking between the U. S. Marshal and another officer, and behind him his brother and his master, so like him that one could hardly be told from the other. The moment they appeared, Harriet roused from her stooping posture, threw up a window, and cried to her friends: "Here he comes--take him!" and then darted down the stairs like a wild-cat. She seized one officer and pulled him down, then another, and tore him away from the man; and keeping her arms about the slave, she cried to her friends: "Drag us out! Drag him to the river! Drown him! but don't let them have him!" They were knocked down together, and while down she tore off her sunbonnet and tied it on the head of the fugitive. When he rose, only his head could be seen, and amid the surging mass of people the slave was no longer recognized, while the master appeared like the slave. Again and again they were knocked down, the poor slave utterly helpless, with his manacled wrists streaming with blood. Harriet's outer clothes were torn from her, and even her stout shoes were all pulled from her feet, yet she never relinquished her hold of the man, till she had dragged him to the river, where he was tumbled into a boat, Harriet following in a ferryboat to the other side. But the telegraph was ahead of them, and as soon as they landed he was seized and hurried from her sight. After a time, some school children came hurrying along, and to her anxious inquiries they answered, "He is up in that house, in the third story." Harriet rushed up to the place. Some men were attempting to make their way up the stairs. The officers were firing down, and two men were lying on the stairs, who had been shot. Over their bodies our heroine rushed, and with the help of others burst open the door of the room, dragged out the fugitive, whom Harriet carried down stairs in her arms. A gentleman who was riding by with a fine horse, stopped to ask what the disturbance meant; and on hearing the story, his sympathies seemed to be thoroughly aroused; he sprang from his wagon, calling out, "That is a blood-horse, drive him till he drops." The poor man was hurried in; some of his friends jumped in after him, and drove at the most rapid rate to Schenectady.

This is the story Harriet told to the writer. By some persons it seemed too wonderful for belief, and an attempt was made to corroborate it. Rev. Henry Fowler, who was at the time at Saratoga, kindly volunteered to go to Troy and ascertain the facts. His report was, that he had had a long interview with Mr. Townsend, who acted during the trial as counsel for the slave, that he had given him a "rich narration," which he would write out the next week for this little book. But before he was to begin his generous labor, and while engaged in some kind efforts for the prisoners at Auburn, he was stricken down by the heat of the sun, and is for a long time debarred from labor.

FUGITIVE SLAVE RESCUE IN TROY
From the Troy Whig, April 28, 1859.

Yesterday afternoon, the streets of this city and West Troy were made the scenes of unexampled excitement. For the first time since the passage of the Fugitive Slave Law, an attempt was made here to carry its provisions into execution, and the result was a terrific encounter between the officers and the prisoner's friends, the triumph of mob law, and the final rescue of the fugitive. Our city was thrown into a grand state of turmoil, and for a time every other topic was forgotten, to give place to this new excitement. People did not think last evening to ask who was nominated at Charleston, or whether the news of the Heenan and Sayers battle had arrived--everything was merged into the fugitive slave case, of which it seems the end is not yet.

Charles Nalle, the fugitive, who was the cause of all this excitement, was a slave on the plantation of B. W. Hansborough, in Culpepper County, Virginia, till the 19th of October, 1858, when he made his escape, and went to live in Columbia, Pennsylvania. A wife and five children are residing there now. Not long since he came to Sandlake, in this county, and resided in the family of Mr. Crosby until about three weeks ago. Since that time, he has been employed as coachman by Uri Gilbert, Esq., of this city. He is about thirty years of age, tall, quite light-complexioned, and good-looking. He is said to have been an excellent and faithful servant.

At Sandlake, we understand that Nalle was often seen by one H. F. Averill, formerly connected with one of the papers of this city, who communicated with his reputed owner in Virginia, and gave the information that led to a knowledge of the whereabouts of the fugitive. Averill wrote letters for him, and thus obtained an acquaintance with his history. Mr. Hansborough sent on an agent, Henry J. Wall, by whom the necessary papers were got out to arrest the fugitive.

Yesterday morning about 11 o'clock, Charles Nalle was sent to procure some bread for the family by whom he was employed. He failed to return. At the baker's, he was arrested by Deputy United States Marshal J. W. Holmes, and immediately taken before United States Commissioner Miles Beach. The son of Mr. Gilbert, thinking it strange that he did not come back, sent to the house of William Henry, on Division Street, where he boarded, and his whereabouts was discovered.

The examination before Commissioner Beach was quite brief. The evidence of Averill and the agent was taken, and the Commissioner decided to remand Nalle to Virginia. The necessary papers were made out and given to the Marshal.

By this time it was two o'clock, and the fact began to be noised abroad that there was a fugitive slave in Mr. Beach's office, corner of State and First Streets. People in knots of ten or twelve collected near the entrance, looking at Nalle, who could be seen at an upper window. William Henry, a colored man, with whom Nalle boarded, commenced talking from the curb-stone in a loud voice to the crowd. He uttered such sentences as, "There is a fugitive slave in that office--pretty soon you will see him come forth. He is going to be taken down South, and you will have a chance to see him. He is to be taken to the depot, to go to Virginia in the first train. Keep watch of those stairs, and you will have a sight." A number of women kept shouting, crying, and by loud appeals excited the colored persons assembled.

Still the crowd grew in numbers. Wagons halted in front of the locality, and were soon piled with spectators. An alarm of fire was sounded, and hose carriages dashed through the ranks of men, women, and boys; but they closed again, and kept looking with expectant eyes at the window where the negro was visible. Meanwhile, angry discussions commenced. Some persons agitated a rescue, and others favored law and order. Mr. Brockway, a lawyer, had his coat torn for expressing his sentiments, and other melees kept the interest alive.

All at once there was a wild hulloa, and every eye was turned up to see the legs and part of the body of the prisoner protruding from the second-story window, at which he was endeavoring to escape. Then arose a shout! "Drop him!" "Catch him!" "Hurrah!" But the attempt was a fruitless one, for somebody in the office pulled Nalle back again, amid the shouts of a hundred pair of lungs. The crowd at this time numbered nearly a thousand persons. Many of them were black, and a good share were of the female sex. They blocked up State Street from First Street to the alley, and kept surging to and fro.

Martin I. Townsend, Esq., who acted as counsel for the fugitive, did not arrive in the Commissioner's office until a decision had been rendered. He immediately went before Judge Gould, of the Supreme Court, and procured a writ of habeas corpus in the usual form, *returnable* immediately. This was given Deputy Sheriff Nathaniel Upham, who at once proceeded to Commissioner Beach's office, and served it on Holmes. Very injudiciously the officers proceeded at once to Judge Gould's office, although it was evident they would have to pass through an excited, unreasonable crowd. As soon as the officers and their prisoner emerged from the door, an old negro, who had been standing at the bottom of the stairs, shouted, "Here they come," and the crowd made a terrific rush at the party.

From the office of Commissioner Beach, in the Mutual Building, to that of Judge Gould, in Congress Street, is less than two blocks, but it was made a regular battle-field. The moment the prisoner emerged from the doorway, in custody of Deputy-Sheriff Upham, Chief of Police Quin, Officers Cleveland and Holmes, the crowd made one grand charge, and those nearest the prisoner seized him violently, with the intention of pulling him away from the officers, but they were foiled; and down First to Congress Street, and up the latter in front of Judge Gould's chambers, went the surging mass. Exactly what did go on in the crowd, it is impossible to say, but the pulling, hauling, mauling, and shouting, gave evidences of frantic efforts on the part of the rescuers, and a stern resistance from the conservators of the law. In front of Judge Gould's office the combat was at its height. No stones or other missiles were used; the battle was fist to fist. We believe an order was given to take the prisoner the other way, and there was a grand rush towards the West, past First and River Streets, as far as Dock Street. All this time there was a continual melee. Many of the officers were hurt-- among them Mr. Upham, whose object was solely to do his duty by taking Nalle before Judge Gould in accordance with the writ of habeas corpus. A number in the crowd were more or less hurt, and it is a wonder that these were not badly injured, as pistols were drawn and chisels used.

The battle had raged as far as the corner of Dock and Congress Streets, and the victory remained with the rescuers at last. The officers were completely worn out with their exertions, and it was impossible to continue their hold upon him any longer. Nalle was at liberty. His friends rushed him down Dock Street to the lower ferry, where there was a skiff lying ready to start. The fugitive was put in, the ferryman rowed off, and amid the shouts of hundreds who fined the banks of the river, Nalle was carried into Albany County.

As the skiff landed in West Troy, a negro sympathizer waded up to the waist, and pulled Nalle out of the boat. He went up the hill alone, however, and there who should he meet but Constable Becker? The latter official seeing a man with manacles on, considered it his duty to arrest him. He did so, and took him in a wagon to the office of Justice Stewart, on the second floor of the corner building near the ferry. The Justice was absent.

When the crowd on the Troy bank had seen Nalle safely landed, it was suggested that he might be recaptured. Then there was another rush made for the steam ferry-boat, which carried over about 400 persons, and left as many more--a few of the latter being soused in their efforts to get on the boat. On landing in West Troy, there, sure enough, was the prisoner, locked up in a strong office, protected by Officers Becker, Brown and Morrison, and the door barricaded.

Not a moment was lost. Up stairs went a score or more of resolute men--the rest "piling in" promiscuously, shouting and execrating the officers. Soon a stone flew against the door--then another--and bang, bang! went off a couple of pistols, but the officers who fired them took good care to aim pretty high. The assailants were forced to retreat for a moment. "They 've got pistols," said one. "Who cares?" was the reply; "they can only kill a dozen of us--come on." More stones and more pistol-shots ensued. At last the door was pulled open by an immense negro, and in a moment he was felled by a hatchet in the hands of Deputy Sheriff Morrison; but the body of the fallen man blocked up the door so that it could not be shut, and a friend of the prisoner pulled him out. Poor fellow! he might well say, "Save me from my friends." Amid the pulling and hauling, the iron had cut his arms, which were bleeding profusely, and he could hardly walk, owing to fatigue.

He has since arrived safely in Canada.

Statements made by Martin I. Townsend, Esq., of Troy, who was counsel for the fugitive, Charles Nalle

Nalle is an octoroon; his wife has the same infusion of Caucasian blood. She was the daughter of her master, and had, with her sister, been bred by him in his family, as his own child. When the father died, both of these daughters were married and had large families of children. Under the highly Christian national laws of "Old Virginny," these children were the slaves of their grandfather. The old man died, leaving a will, whereby he manumitted his daughters and their children, and provided for the purchase of the freedom of their husbands. The manumission of the children and grandchildren took effect; but the estate was insufficient to purchase the husbands of his daughters, and the father of his grandchildren. The manumitted, by another Christian, "conservative," and "national" provision of law, were forced to leave the State, while the slave husbands remained in slavery. Nalle and his brother-in-law were allowed for a while to visit their families outside Virginia about once a year, but were at length ordered to provide themselves with new wives, as they would be allowed to visit their former ones no more. It was after this that Nalle and his brother-in-law started for the land of freedom, guided by the steady light of the north star. Thank God, neither family now need fear any earthly master or the bay of the blood-hound dogging their fugitive steps.

Nalle returned to Troy with his family about July, 1860, and resided with them there for more than seven years. They are all now residents of the city of Washington, D. C. Nalle and his family are persons of refined manners, and of the highest respectability. Several of his children are red-haired, and a stranger would discover no trace of African blood in their complexions or features. It was the head of this family whom H. F. Averill proposed to doom to returnless exile and lifelong slavery.

When Nalle was brought from Commissioner Beach's office into the street, Harriet Tubman, who had been standing with the excited crowd, rushed amongst the foremost to Nalle, and running one of her arms around his manacled arm, held on to him without ever loosening her hold through the more than half-hour's struggle to Judge Gould's office, and from Judge Gould's office to the dock, where Nalle's liberation was accomplished. In the melee, she was repeatedly beaten over the head with policemen's clubs, but she never for a moment released her hold, but cheered Nalle and his friends with her voice, and struggled with the officers until they were literally worn out with their exertions, and Nalle was separated from them.

True, she had strong and earnest helpers in her struggle, some of whom had white faces as well as human hearts, and are now in Heaven. But she exposed herself to the fury of the sympathizers with slavery, without fear, and suffered their blows without flinching. Harriet crossed the river with the crowd, in the ferry-boat, and when the men who led the assault upon the door of Judge Stewart's office, were stricken down, Harriet and a number of other colored women rushed over their bodies, brought Nalle out, and putting him in the first wagon passing, started him for the West.

A livery team, driven by a colored man, was immediately sent on to relieve the other, and Nalle was seen about Troy no more until he returned a free man by purchase from his master. Harriet also disappeared, and the crowd dispersed. How she came to be in Troy that day, is entirely unknown to our citizens; and where she hid herself after the rescue, is equally a mystery. But her struggle was in the sight of a thousand, perhaps of five thousand spectators.

This woman of whom you have been reading is poor, and partially disabled from her injuries; yet she supports cheerfully and uncomplainingly herself and her old parents, and always has several poor children in her house, who are dependent entirely upon her exertions. At present she has three of these children for whom she is providing, while their parents are working to pay back money borrowed to bring them on. She also maintains by her exertions among the good people of Auburn, two schools of freedmen at the South, providing them teachers and sending them clothes and books. She never asks for anything for herself, but she does ask the charity of the public for "her people."

> For them her tears will fall,
> For them her prayers ascend;
> To them her toils and cares be given,
> Till toils and cares will end.

If any persons are disposed to aid her in her benevolent efforts, they may send donations to Rev. S. M. Hopkins, Professor in the Auburn Theological Seminary, who will make such disposition of the funds sent as may be designated by the donors.

APPENDIX

A few circumstances having come out in conversation with Harriet, they are added here, as they may be of interest to the reader.

On asking Harriet particularly as to the age of her mother, she answered, "Well, I'll tell you, Missis. Twenty-three years ago, in Maryland, I paid a lawyer $5 to look up the will of my mother's first master. He looked back sixty years, and said it was time to give up. I told him to go back furder." He went back sixty-five years, and there he found the will--giving the girl Ritty to his grand-daughter (Mary Patterson), to serve her and her offspring till she was forty-five years of age. This grand-daughter died soon after, unmarried; and as there was no provision for Ritty, in case of her death, she was actually emancipated at that time. But no one informed her of the fact, and she and her dear children remained in bondage till emancipated by the courage and determination of this heroic daughter and sister. The old woman must then, it seems, be ninety-eight years of age, and the old man has probably numbered as many years. And yet these old people, living out beyond the toll-gate, on the South Street road, Auburn, come in every Sunday--more than a mile--to the Central Church. To be sure, deep slumbers settle down upon them as soon as they are seated, which continue undisturbed till the congregation is dismissed; but they have done their best, and who can doubt that they receive a blessing. Immediately after this they go to class-meeting at the Methodist Church. Then they wait for a third service, and after that start out home again.

On asking Harriet where they got anything to eat on Sunday, she said, in her quiet way, "Oh! de ole folks nebber eats anyting on *Sunday,* Missis! We nebber has no food to get for dem on Sunday. Dey always fasts; and dey nebber eats anyting on Fridays. Good Friday, an' five Fridays hand gwine from Good Friday, my fader nebber eats or drinks, all day--fasting for de five bleeding wounds ob Jesus. All the oder Fridays ob de year he nebber eats till de sun goes down; den he takes a little tea an' a piece ob bread." "But is he a Roman Catholic, Harriet?" "Oh no, Misses; he does it for *conscience;* we was taught to do so down South. He says if he denies himself for the sufferings of his Lord an' Master, Jesus will sustain him."

It has been mentioned that Harriet never asks anything for herself, but whenever her people were in trouble, or she felt impelled to go South to guide to freedom friend or brother, or father and mother, if she had not time to work for the money, she was persistent till she got it from somebody. When she received one of her *intimations* that the old people were in trouble, and it was time for her to go to them, she asked the Lord where she should go for the money. She was in some way, as she supposed, directed to the office of a certain gentleman in New York. When she left the house of her friends to go there, she said, "I'm gwine to Mr.--'s office, an' I ain't gwine to lebe there, an' I ain't gwine to eat or drink till I git enough money to take me down after the ole people."

She went into this gentleman's office.

"What do you want, Harriet?" was the first greeting.

"I want some money, sir."

"You do? How much do you want?"

"I want twenty dollars, sir."

"Twenty dollars? Who told you to come here for twenty dollars?"

"De Lord tole me, sir."

"Well, I guess the Lord's mistaken this time."

"I guess he isn't, sir. Anyhow I'm gwine to sit here till I git it."

So she sat down and went to sleep. All the morning and all the afternoon she sat there still, sleeping and rousing up--sometimes finding the office full of gentlemen--sometimes finding herself alone. Many fugitives were passing through Now York at that time, and those who came in supposed that she was one of them, tired out and resting. Sometimes she would be roused up with the words, "Come, Harriet, you had better go. There's no money for you here." "No, sir. I'm not gwine till I git my twenty dollars."

She does not know all that happened, for deep sleep fell upon her; but probably her story was whispered about, and she roused at last to find herself the happy possessor of *sixty dollars,* which had been raised among those who came into the office. She went on her way rejoicing, to bring her old parents from the land of bondage. She found that her father was to be tried the next Monday, for helping off slaves; so, as she says, she "removed his trial to a higher court," and hurried him off to Canada. One more little incident, which, it is hoped, may not be offensive to the young lady to whom it alludes, may be mentioned here, showing Harriet's extreme delicacy in asking anything for herself. Last winter ('67 and '68), as we all know, the snow was very deep for months, and Harriet and the old people were completely snowed-in in their little home. The old man was laid up with rheumatism, and Harriet could not leave home for a long time to procure supplies of corn, if she could have made her way into the city. At length, stern necessity compelled her to plunge through the drifts to the city, and she appeared at the house of one of her firm and fast friends, and was directed to the room of one of the young ladies. She began to walk up and down, as she always does when in trouble. At length she said, "Miss Annie?" "What, Harriet?" A long pause; then again, "Miss Annie?" "Well, what *is* it, Harriet?" This was repeated four times, when the young lady, looking up, saw her eyes filled with tears. She then insisted on knowing what she wanted. And with a great effort, she said, "Miss Annie, could you lend me a quarter till Monday? I never asked it before." Kind friends immediately supplied all the wants of the family, but on Monday Harriet appeared with the quarter she had borrowed.

But though so timid for herself, she is bold enough when the wants of her race are concerned. Even now, while friends are trying to raise the means to publish this little book for her, *she* is going around with the greatest zeal and interest to raise a subscription for her Freedmen's Fair. She called on Hon. Wm. H. Seward, the other day, for a subscription to this object. He said, "Harriet, you have worked for others long enough. It is time you should think of yourself. If you ask for a donation for *yourself,* I will give it to you; but I will not help you to rob yourself for others."

Harriet's charity for all the human race is unbounded. It embraces even the slaveholder-- it sympathizes even with Jeff. Davis, and rejoices at his departure to other lands, with some prospect of peace for the future. She says, "I tink dar's many a slaveholder 'll git to Heaven. Dey don't know no better. Dey acts up to de light dey hab. You take dat sweet little child (pointing to a lonely baby)–'pears more like an angel dan anyting else--take her down dere, let her nebber know nothing 'bout niggers but they was made to be whipped, an' she 'll grow up to use the whip on 'em jus' like de rest. No, Missus, its because dey don't know no better." May God give the people to whom the story of this woman shall come, a like charity, so that through their kindness the last days of her stormy and troubled life may be calm and peaceful.

ESSAY ON WOMAN-WHIPPING

THE subject of the preceding memoir appears to have retained all her life a feeling recollection of the effects of the whip in the hands of her youthful mistress. Considering the vigor and frequency of the application, this is not strange. Infinite cuffs and thwacks, more or less, pass into oblivion; but a flogging with a raw-hide is not easily forgotten. A slave's experience of the whip, however, was not confined to his or to *her* early days. A slave race must be controlled by fear and pain: and the discipline, it was naturally thought, could not begin too early. From childhood to old age they were liable to stripes, for any reason or for no reason. If the slave was guilty of no fault, he might be whipped, as appears from the preceding narrative, merely to impress him with a salutary sense of the master's right and disposition to whip.

A Northern man, born and bred under the influences of freedom and the protection of law, and made acquainted with slavery in its old palmy days, can never forget his sensations at his first sight of a slave-whipping. The utmost he has ever seen in the way of corporal punishment has been the switching of some obstreperous child by competent authority; a discipline administered with prudence and moderation; drawing no blood and leaving no scar. He now sees an adult person stripped to the skin, his arms tied at their utmost stretch above his head, or across some object which binds him into a posture the best adapted to feel the full force of each blow. The instrument of suffering is not a birch twig or a ferule, but a twisted raw-hide, or heavy "black snake;" either of them highly effective weapons in the hands of a stout executioner. Our Northern novice stands horror-stricken and paralyzed for a moment; but at the second or third blow, and the piteous scream of *Oh Lord! Massa!* which follows, he digs his fingers into his ears, and rushes to the furthest corner of his tent or dwelling, to escape the scene. Even if he *could* have endured the sight and sound a while longer, he dared not. The horror in his face, and perhaps the irrepressible word or act of interference was too sure to bring upon himself the vengeance due to a "d--d Abolitionist." The little knot of Southern *habitués* look on with critical inspection, squirting tobacco-juice, with their hands in their pockets.

If the subject is a woman, the interest rises higher, and the crowd would be greater. There is a refinement of cruelty in the whipping of a woman which used to stimulate agreeably the dull sensibilities of a Southern mob. A dish of torture had to be peppered very high to please the palates of those epicures in brutality. The helplessness and terror of the victim, the exposure of her person, the opportunity for coarse jests at her expense, all combined to make it a scene of rare enjoyment. How the "chivalric" mind can endure the loss of such gratifications it is difficult to conceive. The Romans were weaned from crucifixions and gladiatorial combats very gradually. The process of ameliorating criminal law and humanizing public sentiment went on for more than two centuries. It was full four hundred years after the epoch of our redemption when the monk Telemachus threw himself between the hired swordsmen, whom a Christian audience was applauding, and laid down his own life to wind up the spectacle. But the bloody morsel has been snatched from the mouths of the "chivalry" at one clutch. No wonder their mortification vents itself in weeping and wailing, and knashing of teeth, and in such miscellaneous atrocities as their "Ku-Klux-Klans" can venture to inflict on helpless freedmen and radicals.[2]

A recent Southern paper (the *Virginia Advertiser*) finds a providential provision for the enslavement of the negro race in the thickness of their skulls, enabling them to bear without injury the blows inflicted in sudden rage by their masters; a suggestive confession, by the way, of the influence of slavery on the tempers of the slaveholders. The whole race must be prepared, it seems, for blows on the head with whatever weapon came to hand! But admitting the thickness of the skulls, it appears from an incident in the preceding pages, as well as from other known instances, that the inventive genius of the slave-whipping chivalry contrived to baffle the humane designs of Providence--a negro skull well padded with wool might bear without injury the blow of a boot-jack or a hammer, and yet prove insufficient to resist the impact or a musket-ball or a ten-pound weight. It is of no avail to plate a vessel with six inches of iron, if she is to be pounded with bolts that can mash an eight-inch armor. Apparently, Divine Providence stopped short of the necessary security for the predestined slave race. It should have arranged for a progressive thickening of the negro cranium to meet the increase of violence on the part of the master; until at length slavery might be encountered with a difficulty like that which besets naval gunnery, viz., what would be the result if an *infrangible* African skull should be beaten by an *irresistable* Caucasian club?

But even this Virginia *laudator temporis acti,* this melancholy mourner at the tomb of defunct slavery, does not allege any such Providential thickening of the negro cuticle as to amount to a satisfactory anæsthesis against whipping. It has never been proven that a Virginia paddle or a Georgia raw-hide well applied did not make the blood spin as freely through a black skin as through a white one; nor has any Southern savant of the Nott and Gliddon school shown that there was not the same *relative* delicacy of organization in the slave woman as in the free. A black woman was, relatively to the black man, the more delicate subject for the whip; something more sensitive to the shame of stripping, more liable to terror, and of rather softer fiber; so that the lash went deeper both into soul and sense than in the case of her sable brother.

And this fact made the black woman a very suitable subject for the whip in the hands of the Southern lady. To succeed in slave-whipping as in any other fine art, the Horatian canon must be regarded, which requires us to take a subject suited to our strength. It would have been unreasonable, in ordinary cases, to expect a "dark-eyed daughter of the South" to flog handsomely a stalwart negro man; she sometimes did it, after he had been well tied up. But the slave girl was exactly suited to her flagellating capacities. A good many women, North as well as South, manifest a tendency to become tyrants in their own households, and love to bully their servants. But this is an evil of a mitigated nature in Northern society. The stupidest "help" in the kitchen knows she is safe from any other lash than her mistress' tongue, and is commonly an adept at the business of answering back again.

But the Southern mistress was a domestic devil with horns and claws; selfish, insolent, accustomed to be waited on for everything. She grew up with the instinct of tyranny--to punish violently the least neglect or disobedience in her servants. The variable temper of girlhood, not ugly unless thwarted, became in the "Southern matron" a chronic fury. She was her own "overseer," and, like that out-door functionary, had her own scepter, which she did not bear in vain. The raw-hide lay upon the shelf within easy reach, and her arm was vigorous with exercise. The breaking of a plate, the spilling of a cup, the misplacing of a pin in her dress, or any other misadventure in the chapter of accidents, was promptly illustrated with numerous cuts. The lash well laid on the shoulders of a black *femme-de-chambre,* or screaming child, was an agreeable titillation of the nervous sensibilities of the languid creole; a headache, or a heartache, transferred itself through the medium of the rawhide to the back of Phillis or Araminta. They no doubt whipped sometimes, like Mr. Squeers, for the mere fun of the thing. It is an exquisite pleasure to a cowardly nature to have some creature to torment; and there is this nemesis about cruelty that it engenders an appetite which, like that for alcoholic stimulents, for ever demands increased indulgence. It was the vindictive woman's nature in the South that protracted and gave added ferocity to the rebellion. These woman-whipping wives and mothers it was who hounded on the masculine chivalry to the work of exterminating the "accursed Yankees," and thus made their own punishment so much sorer than it need have been.

The mention of these amiable Southern characteristics cannot fail to recall that highly suggestive scene of the Malebolge, with the illustration of Gustave Doré, in which the tempters and destroyers of women are seen scourged with whips, in the hands of demons; especially when we remember that the whipping of slave women to make them consent to their own dishonor, was one of the usages of the patriarchal chivalry. There is not a scene in which the imaginings of Dante have been better seconded by the pencil of the great French artist: the flying wretches hurrying in opposite directions, as the crowds in the Jubilee year trampled each other, going and returning across the St. Angelo Bridge; among them the bat-winged fiends with whips, lashing right and left! In the throng are female figures: women who in life tortured and corrupted other women. What terror in face an attitude! How desperately they grapple with the rocks to lift themselves out of reach of the scourge! And these two demons in the foreground! What an absolute idealization of muscular ferocity! Every sinewy line in their cantour displays the force of a fallen demi-god; their very tails curl with delight in their ministry of vengeance.

> Ah! come facen levar le berze,
> Alle prime percosse, e gia nessuno,
> Le second aspettava ne le terze!

Ah! how they make them skip! There is Legree and Tom Gordon, and Madame de Schlangenbad, from Louisiana, and Mrs. Crawley (*née* Sharp) from South Carolina, squirming under the torture! A very instructive, if not agreeable exhibition!

But this fury in celestial Southern bosoms was merely institutional. Dip the gentlest nature into the element of irresponsible power, and it becomes in time covered over with a foul incrustation of cruelty. Those beastly Roman ladies of Juvenal's time, who could order a slave woman to be whipped to death without condeseending to give any other reason than their *sic volo, sic jubeo,* were not naturally worse than others. Take any Roman or Southern girl of ten years of age, put a whip in her hands, and a helpless slave child at her mercy; let her see nothing but brutality to inferiors all around her, and by the time she is ready to be married, she can hold up her thumb to the standing gladiator in the arena, or beg her lover to bring her back from Bull Run a ring from the bones of some Yankee soldier. It is a publicly known private fact, illustrative of the influence of slavery on the female character, that when a certain Northern clergyman applied to her father for the hand of a celebrated Maryland heiress, the reply was, "You are quite welcome to her! but I think it only fair to tell you that if I were going to storm hell, I should put her in the advance."

There is every reason to hope, therefore, that the Southern character, both male and female, will become gradually ameliorated by the changed condition under which it will hereafter be formed. It is a common error, one in which the Southern people themselves share, that there is something in their climate to nurse and to justify their "high spirit," *anglicé* their quarrelsomeness and brutality of temper. It is very pleasant to lay off upon Nature or Providence what belongs only to will or institutions. A man indulges in violent passions with little restraint or remorse, so long as he can persuade himself he is merely what certain positive natural laws make him. What an opiate for a conscience defiled with lust and blood, to think that this is only natural to the "sunny South." But in fact, the people of warm, temperate, and tropical regions are most commonly gentle of mood; the climate acts as an anodyne, and soothes them into a peaceful equilibrium of the passions. The negroes of the Southern States are not passionate or vindictive--well for their late masters and present persecutors that they are not! What they may become from the treatment they are experiencing from those preternatural and predestinated fools, is another question.

The only reason the "chivalry" are bad-tempered and quarrelsome, is found in that despotism in which they have been nursed, and which associates the idea of personal dignity with an instant resort to violence at any contradiction. But for slavery, the people of Mississippi would have been no more addicted to street fights, dueling, midnight assassinations, etc., than the people of Massachusetts. That the former have any advantage in respect to courage, has been sufficiently disproved by the rebellion. Whether the ex-Confederate ladies may or may not be able to "fire the Southern heart" for another attempt to overthrow the Government, it will at least never be done under the persuasion that one Southerner is equal to five or any other number above unity, of Yankees.

The traditions of slavery, indeed, will remain to keep alive among the late slaveholding caste, the insolent and unchristian temper on which they have prided themselves. But having no more helpless pendants to storm at and abuse, their valor will needs submit to gradual modifications. Some degree of self-government will become a necessity. It may require several generations;

but *institutions* ceasing to corrupt them, the loss of wealth, the necessity of work and a new Gospel of peace, better than their old slaveholding Christianity, will gradually educate them into a law-abiding, orderly, and virtuous people.

The Southern woman will of course share early in this beneficent change--no longer perverted into a she-devil by the possession of unrestrained power, and paying just wages to servants, who, if not suited with their work, can leave without having to run off; her gentler virtues will have a chance to assert themselves. Her striking qualities will subside into a charming vivacity of temper. She will become a gracious and pious mater-familias; she will perhaps in time learn to apply to her own children a portion of that discipline of which her slaves enjoyed a monopoly. In short, there neither is nor ever was any reason, slavery excepted, why the Southern whites should not possess a character for industry, peacefulness, and religion, equal to that of the rural districts of New York and New England.

Thank God that we have lived to see such awful barbarisms extinct! In fifty years the last woman-whipper at the South will be as dead as Cleopatra; as dead as the pre-Adamite brute organizations. History will be ashamed to record their doings. The fictions in which they are enbalmed will be lost in the better coming era of morals and letters. By the time the South has been overflowed and regenerated by a beneficent inundation of Northern "carpet-baggers," with Yankee capital and enterprise, it will be forgotten that a race capable of the crimes referred to in the preceding story, ever existed.

Harriet: The Moses of Her People

"Farewell, ole Marster, don't think hard of me,
    I'm going on to Canada, where all de slaves are free."

"Jesus, Jesus will go wid you,
        He will lead you to His throne,
    He who died has gone before you,
        Trod de wine-press all alone."

PREFACE

The title I have given my black heroine, in this second edition of her story, viz.: THE MOSES OF HER PEOPLE, may seem a little ambitious, considering that this Moses was a woman, and that she succeeded in piloting only three or four hundred slaves from the land of bondage to the land of freedom.

But I only give her here the name by which she was familiarly known, both at the North and the South, during the years of terror of the Fugitive Slave Law, and during our last Civil War, in both of which she took so prominent a part.

And though the results of her unexampled heroism were not to free a whole nation of bond-men and bond-women, yet this object was as much the desire of her heart, as it was of that of the great leader of Israel. Her cry to the slave-holders, was ever like his to Pharaoh, "Let my people go!" and not even he imperiled life and limb more willingly, than did our courageous and self-sacrificing friend.

Her name deserves to be handed down to posterity, side by side with the names of Jeanne D'Arc, Grace Darling, and Florence Nightingale, for not one of these women, noble and brave as they were, has shown more courage, and power of endurance, in facing danger and death to relieve human suffering, than this poor black woman, whose story I am endeavoring in a most imperfect way to give you.

Would that Mrs. Stowe had carried out the plan she once projected, of being the historian of our sable friend; by her graphic pen, the incidents of such a life might have been wrought up into a tale of thrilling interest, equaling, if not exceeding her world renowned "Uncle Tom's Cabin."

The work fell to humbler hands, and the first edition of this story, under the title of "Harriet Tubman," was written in the greatest possible haste, while the writer was preparing for a voyage to Europe. There was pressing need for this book, to save the poor woman's little home from being sold under a mortgage, and letters and facts were penned down rapidly, as they came in. The book has now been in part re-written and the letters and testimonials placed in an appendix.

For the satisfaction of the incredulous (and there will naturally be many such, when so strange a tale is repeated to them), I will here state that so far as it has been possible, I have received corroboration of every incident related to me by my heroic friend. I did this for the satisfaction of others, not for my own. No one can hear Harriet talk, and not believe every word she says. As Mr. Sanborn says of her, "she is too *real* a person, not to be true."

Many incidents quite as wonderful as those related in the story, I have rejected, because I had no way in finding the persons who could speak to their truth.

This woman was the friend of William H. Seward, of Gerritt Smith, of Wendell Phillips, of William Lloyd Garrison, and of many other distinguished philanthropists before the War, as of very many officers of the Union Army during the conflict.

After her almost superhuman efforts in making her own escape from slavery, and then re-turning to the South *nineteen times*, and bringing away with her over three hundred fugitives, she was sent by Governor Andrew of Massachusetts to the South at the beginning of the War, to act as spy and scout for our armies, and to be employed as hospital nurse when needed.

Here for four years she labored without any remuneration, and during the time she was acting as nurse, never drew but twenty days' rations from our Government. She managed to support herself, as well as to take care of the suffering soldiers.

Secretary Seward exerted himself in every possible way to procure her a pension from Congress, but red-tape proved too strong even for him, and her case was rejected, because it did not come under any recognized law.

The first edition of this little story was published through the liberality of Gerritt Smith, Wendell Phillips, and prominent men in Auburn, and the object for which it was written was accomplished. But that book has long been out of print, and the facts stated there are all unknown to the present generation. There have, I am told, often been calls for the book, which could not be answered, and I have been urged by many friends as well as by Harriet herself, to prepare another edition. For another necessity has arisen and she needs help again not for herself, but for certain helpless ones of her people.

Her own sands are nearly run, but she hopes, 'ere she goes home, to see this work, a hospital, well under way. Her last breath and her last efforts will be spent in the cause of those for whom she has already risked so much.

> For them her tears will fall,
>> For them her prayers ascend;
>> To them her toils and cares be given,
>> Till toils and cares shall end.
>
>>> S.H.B.

Letter from Mr. Oliver Johnson for the second edition:

NEW YORK, *March 6*, 1886.

MY DEAR MADAM:

I am very glad to learn that you are about to publish a revised edition of your life of that heroic woman, Harriet Tubman, by whose assistance so many American slaves were enabled to break their bonds.

During the period of my official connection with the Anti-Slavery office in New York, I saw her frequently, when she came there with the companies of slaves, whom she had successfully piloted away from the South; and often listened with wonder to the story of her adventures and hair-breadth escapes.

She always told her tale with a modesty which showed how unconscious she was of having done anything more than her simple duty. No one who listened to her could doubt her perfect truthfulness and integrity.

Her shrewdness in planning the escape of slaves, her skill in avoiding arrest, her courage in every emergency, and her willingness to endure hardship and face any danger for the sake of her poor followers was phenomenal.

I regret to hear that she is poor and ill, and hope the sale of your book will give her the relief she so much needs and so well deserves.

Yours truly,

OLIVER JOHNSON.

AUBURN THEOL. SEMINARY,
March 16, 1886.

By PROFESSOR HOPKINS

The remarkable person who is the subject of the following sketch, has been residing mostly ever since the close of the war in the outskirts of the City of Auburn, during all which time I have been well acquainted with her. She has all the characteristics of the pure African race strongly marked upon her, though from which one of the various tribes that once fed the Barracoons, on the Guinea coast, she derived her indomitable courage and her passionate love of freedom I know not; perhaps from the Fellatas, in whom those traits were predominant.

Harriet lives upon a farm which the twelve hundred dollars given her by Mrs. Bradford from the proceeds of the first edition of this little book, enabled her to redeem from a mortgage held by the late Secretary Seward.

Her household is very likely to consist of several old black people, "bad with the rheumatize," some forlorn wandering woman, and a couple of small images of God cut in ebony. How she manages to feed and clothe herself and them, the Lord best knows. She has too much pride and too much faith to beg. She takes thankfully, but without any great effusiveness of gratitude, whatever God's messengers bring her.

I have never heard that she absolutely lacked. There are some good people in various parts of the country, into whose hearts God sends the thought, from time to time, that Harriet may be at the bottom of the flour sack, or of the potatoes, and the "help in time of need" comes to her.

Harriet's simplicity and ignorance have, in some cases, been imposed upon, very signally in one instance in Auburn, a few years ago; but nobody who knows her has the slightest doubt of her perfect integrity.

The following sketch taken by Mrs. Bradford, chiefly from Harriet's own recollections, which are wonderfully distinct and minute, but also from other corroborative sources, gives but a very imperfect account of what this woman has been.

Her color, and the servile condition in which she was born and reared, have doomed her to obscurity, but a more heroic soul did not breathe in the bosom of Judith or of Jeanne D'Arc.

No fear of the lash, the blood-hound, or the fiery stake, could divert her from her self-imposed task of leading as many as possible of her people "from the land of Egypt, from the house of bondage."

The book is good literature for the black race, or the white race, and though no similar conditions may arise, to test the possibilities that are in any of them, yet the example of this poor slave woman may well stand out before them, and before all people, black or white, to show what a lofty and martyr spirit may accomplish, struggling against overwhelming obstacles.

HARRIET, THE MOSES OF HER PEOPLE

On a hot summer's day, perhaps sixty years ago, a group of merry little darkies were rolling and tumbling in the sand in front of the large house of a Southern planter. Their shining skins gleamed in the sun, as they rolled over each other in their play, and their voices, as they chattered together, or shouted in glee, reached even to the cabins of the negro quarter, where the old people groaned in spirit, as they thought of the future of those unconscious young revelers; and their cry went up, "O, Lord, how long!"

Apart from the rest of the children, on the top rail of a fence, holding tight on to the tall gate post, sat a little girl of perhaps thirteen years of age; darker than any of the others, and with a more decided *woolliness* in the hair; a pure unmitigated African. She was not so entirely in a state of nature as the rollers in the dust beneath her; but her only garment was a short woolen skirt, which was tied around her waist, and reached about to her knees. She seemed a dazed and stupid child, and as her head hung upon her breast, she looked up with dull blood-shot eyes towards her young brothers and sisters, without seeming to see them. Bye and bye the eyes closed, and still clinging to the post, she slept. The other children looked up and said to each other, "Look at Hatt, she's done gone off agin!" Tired of their present play ground they trooped off in another direction, but the girl slept on heavily, never losing her hold on the post, or her seat on her perch. Behold here, in the stupid little negro girl, the future deliverer of hundreds of her people; the spy and scout of the Union armies; the devoted hospital nurse; the protector of hunted fugitives; the eloquent speaker in public meetings; the cunning eluder of pursuing man-hunters; the heaven guided pioneer through dangers seen and unseen; in short, as she has well been called, "The Moses of her People."

Here in her thirteenth year she is just recovering from the first terrible effects of an injury inflicted by her master, who in an ungovernable fit of rage threw a heavy weight at the unoffending child, breaking in her skull, and causing a pressure upon her brain, from which in her old age she is suffering still. This pressure it was which caused the fits of somnolency so frequently to come upon her, and which gave her the appearance of being stupid and half-witted in those early years. But that brain which seemed so dull was full of busy thoughts, and her life problem was already trying to work itself out there.

She had heard the shrieks and cries of women who were being flogged in the negro quarter; she had listened to the groaned out prayer, "Oh, Lord, have mercy!" She had already seen two older sisters taken away as part of a chain gang, and they had gone no one knew whither; she had seen the agonized expression on their faces as they turned to take a last look at their "Old Cabin Home;" and had watched them from the top of the fence, as they went off weeping and lamenting, till they were hidden from her sight forever. She saw the hopeless grief of the poor old mother, and the silent despair of the aged father, and already she began to revolve in her mind the question, "Why should such things be?" "Is there no deliverance for my people?"

The sun shone on, and Harriet still slept seated on the fence rail. They, those others, had no anxious dreams of the future, and even the occasional sufferings of the present time caused them but a temporary grief. Plenty to eat, and warm sunshine to bask in, were enough to constitute their happiness; Harriet, however, was not one of these. God had a great work for her to do in the world, and the discipline and hardship through which she passed in her early years, were only preparing her for her after life of adventure and trial; and through these to come out as the Savior and Deliverer of her people, when she came to years of womanhood.

As yet she had seen no "visions," and heard no "voices;" no foreshadowing of her life of toil and privation, of flight before human blood-hounds, of watchings, and hidings, of perils by land, and perils by sea, yea, and of perils by false brethren, or of miraculous deliverance had yet come to her. No hint of the great mission of her life, to guide her people from the land of bondage to the land of freedom. But, "Why should such things be?" and "Is there no help?" These were the questions of her waking hours.

The dilapidated state of things about the "Great House" told truly the story of waning fortunes, and poverty was pressing upon the master. One by one the able-bodied slaves disappeared; some were sold, others hired to other masters. No questions were asked; no information given; they simply disappeared. A "lady," for so she was designated, came driving up to the great house one day, to see if she could find there a young girl to take care of a baby. The lady wished to pay low wages, and so the most stupid and the most incapable of the children on the plantation was chosen to go with her. Harriet, who could command less wages than any other child of her age on the plantation, was therefore put into the wagon without a word of explanation, and driven off to the lady's house. It was not a very fine house, but Harriet had never before been in any dwelling better than the cabins of the negro quarter.

She was engaged as child's nurse, but she soon found that she was expected to be maid of all work by day, as well as child's nurse by night. The first task that was set her was that of sweeping and dusting a parlor. No information was vouchsafed as to the manner of going about this work, but she had often swept out the cabin, and this part of her task was successfully accomplished. Then at once she took the dusting cloth, and wiped off tables, chairs and mantel-piece. The dust, as dust will do, when it has nowhere else to go, at once settled again, and chairs and tables were soon covered with a white coating, telling a terrible tale against Harriet, when her Mistress came in to see how the work progressed. Reproaches, and savage words, fell upon the ears of the frightened child, and she was commanded to do the work all over again. It was done in precisely the same way, as before, with the same result. Then the whip was brought into requisition, and it was laid on with no light hand. Five times before breakfast this process was repeated, when a new actor appeared upon the scene. Miss Emily, a sister of the Mistress, had been roused from her morning slumber by the sound of the whip, and the screams of the child; and being of a less imperious nature than her sister, she had come in to try to set matters right.

"Why do you whip the child, Susan, for not doing what she has never been taught to do? Leave her to me a few minutes, and you will see that she will soon learn how to sweep and dust a room." Then Miss Emily instructed the child to open the windows, and sweep, then to leave the room, and set the table, while the dust settled; and after that to return and wipe it off. There was no more trouble of that kind. A few words might have set the matter right before; but in those days many a poor slave suffered for the stupidity and obstinacy of a master or mistress, more stupid than themselves.

When the labors, unremitted for a moment, of the long day were over (for this mistress was an economical woman, and intended to get the worth of her money to the uttermost farthing), there was still no rest for the weary child, for there was a cross baby to be rocked continuously, lest it should wake and disturb the mother's rest. The black child sat beside the cradle of the white child, so near the bed, that the lash of the whip would reach her if she ventured for a moment to forget her fatigues and sufferings in sleep. The Mistress reposed upon her bed with the whip on a little shelf over her head. People of color are, unfortunately, so constituted that even if the pressure of a broken skull does not cause a sleep like the sleep of the dead, the need of rest, and the refreshment of slumber after a day of toil, were often felt by them. No doubt, this was a great wrong to their masters, and a cheating them of time which belonged to them, but their slaves did not always look upon it in that light, and tired nature would demand her rights; and so nature and the Mistress had a fight for it.

Rock, rock, went the cradle, and mother and child slept; but alas! the little black hand would sometimes slip down, and the head would droop, and a dream of home and mother would visit the weary one, only to be roughly dispelled by the swift descent of the stinging lash, for the baby had cried out and the mother had been awakened. This is no fictitious tale. That poor neck is even now covered with the scars which sixty years of life have not been able to efface. It may be that she was thus being prepared by the long habit of enforced wakefulness, for the night watches in the woods, and in dens and caves of the earth, when the pursuers were on her track, and the terrified ones were trembling in her shadow. We do not thank *you* for this, cruel woman! for if you did her a service, you did it ignorantly, and only for your own gratification.

But Harriet's powers of endurance failed at last, and she was returned to her
scarred wreck, nothing but skin and bone, with the words that "She wasn't w

The poor old mother nursed her back to life, and her naturally good con
itself, so that as she grew older she began to show signs of the wonderful
after years, when the fugitive slave law was in operation in New York State, enab
a man from the officers who had him in charge, and while numbers were pursuing her, an
the shot was flying like hail about her head, to bear him in her own strong arms beyond the
reach of danger.

As soon as she was strong enough for work, Harriet was hired out to a man whose tyranny
was worse, if possible, than that of the woman she had left. Now it was out of door drudgery
which was put upon her. The labor of the horse and the ox, the lifting of barrels of flour and
other heavy weights were given to her; and powerful men often stood astonished to see this
woman perform feats of strength from which they shrunk incapable. This cruelty she looks
upon as a blessing in disguise (a very questionable shape the blessing took, methinks), for by
it she was prepared for after needs.

Still the pressure upon the brain continued, and with the weight half lifted, she would drop
off into a state of insensibility, from which even the lash in the hand of a strong man could not
rouse her. But if they had only known it, the touch of a gentle hand upon her shoulder, and
her name spoken in tones of kindness, would have accomplished what cruelty failed to do.

The day's work must be accomplished, whether the head was racked with pain, and the frame
was consumed by fever, or not; but the day came at length when poor Harriet could work no
more. The sting of the lash had no power to rouse her now, and the new master finding her
a dead weight on his hands, returned the useless piece of property to him who was called her
"owner." And while she lay there helpless, this man was bringing other men to look at her, and
offering her for sale at the lowest possible price; at the same time setting forth her capabilities,
if once she were strong and well again.

Harriet's religious character I have not yet touched upon. Brought up by parents possessed
of strong faith in God, she had never known the time, I imagine, when she did not trust Him,
and cling to Him, with an all-abiding confidence. She seemed ever to feel the Divine Presence
near, and she talked with God "as a man talketh with his friend." Hers was not the religion of
a morning and evening prayer at stated times, but when she felt a need, she simply told God
of it, and trusted Him to set the matter right.

"And so," she said to me, "as I lay so sick on my bed, from Christmas till March, I was always
praying for poor ole master. 'Pears like I didn't do nothing but pray for ole master. 'Oh, Lord,
convert ole master;' 'Oh, dear Lord, change dat man's heart, and make him a Christian.' And
all the time he was bringing men to look at me, and dey stood there saying what dey would give,
and what dey would take, and all I could say was, 'Oh, Lord, convert ole master.' Den I heard
dat as soon as I was able to move I was to be sent with my brudders, in the chain-gang to de
far South. Then I changed my prayer, and I said, 'Lord, if you ain't never going to change dat
man's heart, *kill him*, Lord, and take him out of de way, so he won't do no more mischief.' Next
ting I heard ole master was dead; and he died just as he had lived, a wicked, bad man. Oh, den
it 'peared like I would give de world full of silver and gold, if I had it, to bring dat pore soul back,
I would give *myself*; I would give eberyting! But he was gone, I couldn't pray for him no more."

As she recovered from this long illness, a deeper religious spirit seemed to take possession
of her than she had ever experienced before. She literally "prayed without ceasing." "'Pears like,
I prayed all de time," she said, "about my work, eberywhere; I was always talking to de Lord.
When I went to the horse-trough to wash my face, and took up de water in my hands, I said,
'Oh, Lord, wash me, make me clean.' When I took up de towel to wipe my face and hands, I
cried, 'Oh, Lord, for Jesus' sake, wipe away all my sins!' When I took up de broom and began
to sweep, I groaned, 'Oh, Lord, whatsoebber sin dere be in my heart, sweep it out, Lord, clar
and clean;' but I can't pray no more for pore ole master." No words can describe the pathos of
her tones as she broke into these words of earnest supplication.

.at was to become of the slaves on this plantation now that the master was dead? Were
⁄ all to be scattered and sent to different parts of the country? Harriet had many brothers and
.sters, all of whom with the exception of the two, who had gone South with the chain-gang,
were living on this plantation, or were hired out to planters not far away. The word passed
through the cabins that another owner was coming in, and that none of the slaves were to be
sold out of the State. This assurance satisfied the others, but it did not satisfy Harriet. Already
the inward monitor was whispering to her, "Arise, flee for your life!" and in the visions of the
night she saw the horsemen coming, and heard the shrieks of women and children, as they
were being torn from each other, and hurried off no one knew whither.

And beckoning hands were ever motioning her to come, and she seemed to see a line dividing
the land of slavery from the land of freedom, and on the other side of that line she saw lovely
white ladies waiting to welcome her, and to care for her. Already in her mind her people were
the Israelites in the land of Egypt, while far away to the north *somewhere*, was the land of Canaan;
but had she as yet any prevision that *she* was to be the Moses who was to be their leader, through
clouds of darkness and fear, and fires of tribulation to that promised land? This she never said.

One day there were scared faces seen in the negro quarter, and hurried whispers passed from
one to another. No one knew how it had come out, but some one had heard that Harriet and
two of her brothers were very soon, perhaps to-day, perhaps to-morrow, to be sent far South
with a gang, bought up for plantation work. Harriet was about twenty or twenty-five years old
at this time, and the constantly recurring idea of escape at *sometime*, took sudden form that
day, and with her usual promptitude of action she was ready to start at once.

She held a hurried consultation with her brothers, in which she so wrought upon their fears,
that they expressed themselves as willing to start with her that very night, for that far North,
where, could they reach it in safety, freedom awaited them. But she must first give some intimation of her purpose to the friends she was to leave behind, so that even if not understood at
the time, it might be remembered afterward as her intended farewell. Slaves must not be seen
talking together, and so it came about that their communication was often made by singing,
and the words of their familiar hymns, telling of the heavenly journey, and the land of Canaan,
while they did not attract the attention of the masters, conveyed to their brethren and sisters in
bondage something more than met the ear. And so she sang, accompanying the words, when
for a moment unwatched, with a meaning look to one and another:

> "When dat ar ole chariot comes,
>   I'm gwine to lebe you,
> I'm boun' for de promised land,
>   Frien's, I'm gwine to lebe you."

Again, as she passed the doors of the different cabins, she lifted up her well-known voice; and
many a dusky face appeared at door or window, with a wondering or scared expression; and
thus she continued:

> "I'm sorry, frien's, to lebe you,
>   Farewell! oh, farewell!
> But I'll meet you in de mornin',
>   Farewell! oh, farewell!
> "I'll meet you in de mornin',
>
>   When you reach de promised land;
> On de oder side of Jordan,
>   For I'm boun' for de promised land."

The brothers started with her, but the way was strange, the north was far away, and all unknown,
the masters would pursue and recapture them, and their fate would be worse than ever before;

and so they broke away from her, and bidding her goodbye, they hastened back to the known horrors of slavery, and the dread of that which was worse.

Harriet was now left alone, but after watching the retreating forms of her brothers, she turned her face toward the north, and fixing her eyes on the guiding star, and committing her way unto the Lord, she started again upon her long, lonely journey. Her farewell song was long remembered in the cabins, and the old mother sat and wept for her lost child. No intimation had been given her of Harriet's intention, for the old woman was of a most impulsive disposition, and her cries and lamentations would have made known to all within hearing Harriet's intended escape. And so, with only the North Star for her guide, our heroine started on the way to liberty, "For," said she, "I had reasoned dis out in my mind; there was one of two things I had a *right* to, liberty, or death; if I could not have one, I would have de oder; for no man should take me alive; I should fight for my liberty as long as my strength lasted, and when de time came for me to go, de Lord would let dem take me."

And so without money, and without friends, she started on through unknown regions; walking by night, hiding by day, but always conscious of an invisible pillar of cloud by day, and of fire by night, under the guidance of which she journeyed or rested. Without knowing whom to trust, or how near the pursuers might be, she carefully felt her way, and by her native cunning, or by God given wisdom, she managed to apply to the right people for food, and sometimes for shelter; though often her bed was only the cold ground, and her watchers the stars of night.

After many long and weary days of travel, she found that she had passed the magic line, which then divided the land of bondage from the land of freedom. But where were the lovely white ladies whom in her visions she had seen, who, with arms outstretched, welcomed her to their hearts and homes. All these visions proved deceitful: she was more alone than ever; but she had crossed the line; no one could take her now, and she would never call any man "Master" more.

"I looked at my hands," she said, "to see if I was de same person now I was free. Dere was such a glory ober eberything, de sun came like gold trou de trees, and ober de fields, and I felt like I was in heaven." But then came the bitter drop in the cup of joy. She was alone, and her kindred were in slavery, and not one of them had the courage to dare what she had dared. Unless she made the effort to liberate them she would never see them more, or even know their fate.

"I knew of a man," she said, "who was sent to the State Prison for twenty-five years. All these years he was always thinking of his home, and counting by years, months, and days, the time till he should be free, and see his family and friends once more. The years roll on, the time of imprisonment is over, the man is free. He leaves the prison gates, he makes his way to his old home, but his old home is not there. The house in which he had dwelt in his childhood had been torn down, and a new one had been put up in its place; his family were gone, their very name was forgotten, there was no one to take him by the hand to welcome him back to life."

"So it was wid me," said Harriet, "I had crossed de line of which I had so long been dreaming. I was free; but dere was no one to welcome me to de land of freedom, I was a stranger in a strange land, and my home after all was down in de old cabin quarter, wid de ole folks, and my brudders and sisters. But to dis solemn resolution I came; I was free, and dey should be free also; I would make a home for dem in de North, and de Lord helping me, I would bring dem all dere. Oh, how I prayed den, lying all alone on de cold, damp ground; 'Oh, dear Lord,' I said, 'I haint got no friend but *you*. Come to my help, Lord, for I'm in trouble!'"

It would be impossible here to give a detailed account of the journeys and labors of this intrepid woman for the redemption of her kindred and friends, during the years that followed. Those years were spent in work, almost by night and day, with the one object of the rescue of her people from slavery. All her wages were laid away with this sole purpose, and as soon as a sufficient amount was secured, she disappeared from her Northern home, and as suddenly and mysteriously she appeared some dark night at the door of one of the cabins on a plantation, where a trembling band of fugitives, forewarned as to time and place, were anxiously awaiting their deliverer. Then she piloted them North, traveling by night, hiding by day, scaling the mountains, fording the rivers, threading the forests, lying concealed as the pursuers passed them.

She, carrying the babies, drugged with paregoric, in a basket on her arm. So she went *nineteen* times, and so she brought away over three hundred pieces of living and breathing "property," with God given souls.

The way was so toilsome over the rugged mountain passes, that often the *men* who followed her would give out, and foot-sore, and bleeding, they would drop on the ground, groaning that they could not take another step. They would lie there and die, or if strength came back, they would return on their steps, and seek their old homes again. Then the revolver carried by this bold and daring pioneer, would come out, while pointing it at their heads she would say, "Dead niggers tell no tales; you go on or die!" And by this heroic treatment she compelled them to drag their weary limbs along on their northward journey.

But the pursuers were after them. A reward of $40,000 was offered by the slave-holders of the region from whence so many slaves had been spirited away, for the head of the woman who appeared so mysteriously, and enticed away their property, from under the very eyes of its owners. Our sagacious heroine has been in the car, having sent her frightened party round by some so-called "Under-ground Railway," and has heard this advertisement, which was posted over her head, read by others of the passengers. She never could read or write herself, but knowing that suspicion would be likely to fall upon any black woman traveling North, she would turn at the next station, and journey towards the South. Who would suspect a fugitive with such a price set upon her head, of rushing at railway speed into the jaws of destruction? With a daring almost heedless, she went even to the very village where she would be most likely to meet one of the masters to whom she had been hired; and having stopped at the Market and bought a pair of live fowls, she went along the street with her sun-bonnet well over her face, and with the bent and decrepit air of an aged, woman. Suddenly on turning a corner, she spied her old master coming towards her. She pulled the string which tied the legs of the chickens; they began to flutter and scream, and as her master passed, she was stooping and busily engaged in attending to the fluttering fowls. And he went on his way, little thinking that he was brushing the very garments of the woman who had dared to steal herself, and others of his belongings.

At one time the pursuit was very close and vigorous. The woods were scoured in all directions, every house was visited, and every person stopped and questioned as to a band of black fugitives, known to be fleeing through that part of the country. Harriet had a large party with her then; the children were sleeping the sound sleep that opium gives; but all the others were on the alert, each one hidden behind his own tree, and silent as death. They had been long without food, and were nearly famished; and as the pursuers seemed to have passed on, Harriet decided to make the attempt to reach a certain "station of the underground railroad" well known to her; and procure food for her starving party. Under cover of the darkness, she started, leaving a cowering and trembling group in the woods, to whom a fluttering leaf, or a moving animal, were a sound of dread, bringing their hearts into their throats. How long she is away! has she been caught and carried off, and if so what is to become of them? Hark! there is a sound of singing in the distance, coming nearer and nearer.

And these are the words of the unseen singer, which I wish I could give you as I have so often heard them sung by herself:

> Hail, oh hail, ye happy spirits,
>   Death no more shall make you fear,
>   Grief nor sorrow, pain nor anguish,
>   Shall no more distress you dere.
> Around Him are ten thousand angels
>
>   Always ready to obey command;
>   Dey are always hovering round you,
>   Till you reach de heavenly land.
> Jesus, Jesus will go wid you,

He will lead you to his throne;
He who died, has gone before you,
Trod de wine-press all alone.
He whose thunders shake creation,

He who bids de planets roll;
He who rides upon the tempest,
And whose scepter sways de whole.
Dark and thorny is de pathway,

Where de pilgrim makes his ways;
But beyond dis vale of sorrow,
Lie de fields of endless days.

The air sung to these words was so wild, so full of plaintive minor strains, and unexpected quavers, that I would defy any white person to learn it, and often as I heard it, it was to me a constant surprise. Up and down the road she passes to see if the coast is clear, and then to make them certain that it is *their* leader who is coming, she breaks out into the plaintive strains of the song, forbidden to her people at the South, but which she and her followers delight to sing together:

Oh go down, Moses,
Way down into Egypt's land,
Tell old Pharaoh,
Let my people go.
Oh Pharaoh said he would go cross,

Let my people go,
And don't get lost in de wilderness,
Let my people go.
Oh go down, Moses,

Way down into Egypt's land,
Tell old Pharaoh,
Let my people go.
You may hinder me here, but you can't up dere,

Let my people go,
He sits in de Hebben and answers prayer,
Let my people go!
Oh go down, Moses,

Way down into Egypt's land,
Tell old Pharaoh,
Let my people go.

And then she enters the recesses of the wood, carrying hope and comfort to the anxious watchers there. One by one they steal out from their hiding places, and are fed and strengthened for another night's journey.

And so by night travel, by signals, by threatenings, by encouragement, through watchings and fastings, and I may say by direct interpositions of Providence, and miraculous deliverances, she brought her people to what was then their land of Canaan; the State of New York. But alas! this State did not continue to be their refuge. For in 1850, I think, the Fugitive Slave

Law was put in force, which bound the people north of Mason and Dixon's line, to return to bondage any fugitive found in their territories.

"After that," said Harriet, "I wouldn't trust Uncle Sam wid my people no longer, but I brought 'em all clar off to Canada."

On her seventh or eighth journey, she brought with her a band of fugitives, among whom was a very remarkable man, whom I knew only by the name of "Joe." Joe was a noble specimen of a negro, enormously tall, and of splendid muscular development. He had been hired out by his master to another planter, for whom he had worked for six years, saving him all the expense of an overseer, and taking all trouble off from his hands. He was such a very valuable piece of property, and had become so absolutely necessary to the planter to whom he was hired, that he determined to buy him at any cost. His old master held him proportionately high. But by paying one thousand dollars down, and promising to pay another thousand in a certain time, the purchase was made, and this chattel passed over into the hands of a new owner.

The morning after the purchase was completed, the new master came riding down on a tall, powerful horse into the negro quarter, with a strong new rawhide in his hand, and stopping before Joe's cabin, called to him to come out. Joe was just eating his breakfast, but with ready obedience, he hastened out at the summons. Slave as he was, and accustomed to scenes of brutality, he was surprised when the order came, "Now, Joe, strip, and take a licking." Naturally enough, he demurred at first, and thought of resisting the order; but he called to mind a scene he had witnessed a few days before in the field, the particulars of which are too horrible to be given here, and he thought it the wisest course to submit; but first he tried a gentle remonstrance.

"Mas'r," said he, "habn't I always been faithful to you? Habn't I worked through sun an' rain, early in de mornin' an' late at night; habn't I saved you an oberseer by doin' his work? hab you anything to complain agin me?"

"No, Joe, I have no complaint to make of you. You're a good nigger, an' you've always worked well. But you belong to *me* now; you're *my* nigger, and the first lesson my niggers have to learn is that I am master and they belong to me, and are never to resist anything I order them to do. So I always begin by giving them a good licking. Now strip and take it."

Joe saw that there was no help for him, and that for the time he must submit. He stripped off his clothing, and took his flogging without a word, but as he drew his shirt up over his torn and bleeding back, he said to himself: "Dis is de first an' de last." As soon as he was able he took a boat, and under cover of the night, rowed down the river, and made his way to the cabin of "Old Ben," Harriet's father, and said to him: "Nex' time *Moses* comes, let me know."

It was not long after this time, that the mysterious woman appeared — the woman on whom no one could lay his finger — and men, women, and children began to disappear from the plantations. One fine morning Joe was missing, and call as loud as he might, the master's voice had no power to bring him forth. Joe had certainly fled; and his brother William was gone, and Peter and Eliza. From other plantations other slaves were missing, and before their masters were awake to the fact, the party of fugitives, following their intrepid leader, were far on their way towards liberty.

The adventures of this escaping party would of themselves fill a volume. They hid in potato holes by day, while their pursuers passed within a few feet of them; they were passed along by friends in various disguises; they scattered and separated; some traveling by boat, some by wagons, some by cars, others on foot, to meet at some specified station of the under-ground railroad. They met at the house of Sam Green,[3] the man who was afterwards sent to prison for ten years for having a copy of "Uncle Tom's Cabin" in his house. And so, hunted and hiding and wandering, they found themselves at last at the entrance of the long bridge which crosses the river at Wilmington, Delaware.

No time had been lost in posting up advertisements and offering rewards for the capture of these fugitives; for Joe in particular the reward offered was very high. First a thousand dollars, then fifteen hundred, and then two thousand, "an' all expenses clar an' clean for his body in Easton Jail." This high reward stimulated the efforts of the officers who were usually on the lookout for escaping fugitives, and the added rewards for others of the party, and the high price set on Harriet's head, filled the woods and highways with eager hunters after human prey. When Harriet and her companions approached the long Wilmington Bridge, a warning was given them by some secret friend, that the advertisements were up, and the bridge was guarded by police officers. Quick as lightning the plans were formed in her ready brain, and the terrified party were separated and hidden in the houses of different friends, till her arrangements for their further journey were completed.

There was at that time residing in Wilmington an old Quaker, whom I may call *my* "friend," for though I never saw his face, I have had correspondence with him in reference to Harriet and her followers. This man, whose name was Thomas Garrett, and who was well known in those days to the friends of the slave, was a man of a wonderfully large and generous heart, through whose hands during those days of distress and horror, no less than three thousand self-emancipated men, women and children passed on their way to freedom. He gave heart, hand, and means to aid these poor fugitives, and to our brave Harriet he often rendered most efficient help in her journeys back and forth.

He was the proprietor of a very large shoe establishment; and not one of these poor travelers aver left his house without a present of a new pair of shoes and other needed help. No sooner had this good man received intelligence of the condition of these poor creatures, than he devised a plan to elude the vigilance of the officers in pursuit, and bring Harriet and her party across the bridge. Two wagons filled with bricklayers were engaged, and sent over; this was a common sight there, and caused no remark. They went across the bridge singing and shouting, and it was not an unexpected thing that they should return as they went. After nightfall (and, fortunately, the night was very dark) the same wagons recrossed the bridge, but with an unlooked-for addition to their party. The fugitives were lying close together on the bottom of the wagons; the bricklayers were on the seats, still singing and shouting; and so they passed the guards, who were all unsuspicious of the nature of the load contained in the wagons, or of the amount of property thus escaping their hands.

The good man, Thomas Garrett, who was in a very feeble state of health when he last wrote me, and has now gone to his reward, supplied them with all needed comforts, and sent them on their way refreshed, and with renewed courage. And Harriet here set up her Ebenezer, saying, "Thus far hath the Lord helped me!" But many a danger, and many a fright, and many a deliverance awaited them, before they reached the city of New York. And even there they were not safe, for the Fugitive Slave Law was in operation, and their only refuge was Canada, which was now their promised land.

They finally reached New York in safety: and this goes almost without saying, for I may as well mention here that of the three hundred and more fugitives whom Harriet piloted from slavery, not one was ever recaptured, though all the cunning and skill of white men, backed by offered rewards of large sums of money, were brought into requisition for their recovery.

As they entered the anti-slavery office in New York, Mr. Oliver Johnson rose up and exclaimed, "Well, Joe, I am glad to see the man who is worth $2,000 to his master." At this Joe's heart sank. "Oh, Mas'r, how did you know me!" he panted. "Here is the advertisement in our office," said Mr. Johnson, "and the description is so close that no one could mistake it." And had he come through all these perils, had he traveled by day and night, and suffered cold and hunger, and lived in constant fear and dread, to find that far off here in New York State, he was recognized at once by the advertisement? How, then, was he ever to reach Canada?

"And how far off is Canada?" he asked. He was shown the map of New York State, and the track of the railroad, for more than three hundred miles to Niagara, where he would cross the river, and be free. But the way seemed long and full of dangers. They were surely safer on their own tired feet, where they might hide in forests and ditches, and take refuge in the friendly underground stations; but here, where this large party would be together in the cars, surely suspicion would fall upon them, and they would be seized and carried back. But Harriet encouraged him in her cheery way. He must not give up now. "De Lord had been with them in six troubles, and he would not desert them in de seventh." And there was nothing to do but to go on. As Moses spoke to the children of Israel, when compassed before and behind by dangers, so she spake to her people, that they should "go forward."

Up to this time, as they traveled they had talked and sung hymns together, like Pilgrim and his friends, and Joe's voice was the loudest and sweetest among them; but now he hanged his harp upon the willows, and could sing the Lord's songs no more.

"From dat time," in Harriet's language, "Joe was silent; he talked no more; he sang no more; he sat wid his head on his hand, an' nobody could 'rouse him, nor make him take any intrust in anything."

They passed along in safety through New York State, and at length found themselves approaching the Suspension Bridge. They could see the promised land on the other side. The uninviting plains of Canada seemed to them,

> "Sweet fields beyond the swelling flood,
> All dressed in living green;"

but they were not safe yet. Until they reached the center of the bridge, they were still in the power of their pursuers, who might at any pause enter the car, and armed with the power of the law, drag them back to slavery. The rest of the party were happy and excited; they were simple, ignorant creatures, and having implicit trust in their leader, they felt safe when with her, and no immediate danger threatened them. But Joe was of a different mould. He sat silent and sad, always thinking of the horrors that awaited him if recaptured. As it happened, all the other passengers were people who sympathized with them, understanding them to be a band of fugitives, and they listened with tears, as Harriet and all except poor Joe lifted up their voices and sang:

> I'm on the way to Canada,
>   That cold and dreary land,
>   De sad effects of slavery,
>   I can't no longer stand;
>   I've served my Master all my days,
>   Widout a dime reward,
>   And now I'm forced to run away,
>   To flee de lash, abroad;
> Farewell, ole Master, don't think hard of me,
> I'm traveling on to Canada, where all de slaves are free.
>   De hounds are baying on my track,
>
>   Ole Master comes behind,
>   Resolved that he will bring me back,
>   Before I cross the line;
>   I'm now embarked for yonder shore,
>   Where a man's *a man* by law,
>   De iron horse will bear me o'er,
>   To "shake de lion's paw;"
> Oh, righteous Father, wilt thou not pity me.
> And help me on to Canada, where all de slaves are free.
>   Oh I heard Queen Victoria say,
>
>   That if we would forsake,
>   Our native land of slavery,
>   And come across de lake;
>   Dat she was standing on de shore,

> Wid arms extended wide,
>> To give us all a peaceful home,
>>> Beyond de rolling tide;
> Farewell, ole Master, don't think hard of me,
> I'm traveling on to Canada, where all de slaves are free.

No doubt the simple creatures with her expected to cross a wide lake instead of a rapid river, and to see Queen Victoria with her crown upon her head, waiting with arms extended wide, to fold them all in her embrace. There was now but "one wide river to cross," and the cars rolled on to the bridge. In the distance was heard the roar of the mighty cataract, and now as they neared the center of the bridge, the falls might be clearly seen. Harriet was anxious to have her companions see this wonderful sight, and succeeded in bringing all to the windows, except Joe. But Joe still sat with his head on his hands, and not even the wonders of Niagara could draw him from his melancholy musings. At length as Harriet knew by the rise of the center of the bridge, and the descent immediately after, the line of danger was passed; she sprang across to Joe's side of the car, and shook him almost out of his seat, as she shouted, "Joe! you've shook de lion's paw!" This was her phrase for having entered on the dominions of England. But Joe did not understand this figurative expression. Then she shook him again, and put it more plainly, "Joe, you're in Queen Victoria's dominions! You're a free man!"

Then Joe arose. His head went up, he raised his hands on high, and his eyes, streaming with tears, to heaven, and then he began to sing and shout:

> "Glory to God and Jesus too,
>> One more soul got safe;
>>> Oh, go and carry the news,
>> One more soul got safe."

"Joe, come and look at the falls!"

> "Glory to God and Jesus too,
>> One more soul got safe."

"Joe! it's your last chance. Come and see de falls!"

> "Glory to God and Jesus too,
>> One more soul got safe."

And this was all the answer. The train stopped on the other side; and the first feet to touch British soil, after those of the conductor, were those of poor Joe.

Loud roared the waters of Niagara, but louder still ascended the Anthem of praise from the overflowing heart of the freeman. And can we doubt that the strain was taken up by angel voices and echoed and re-echoed through the vaults of heaven:

> Glory to God in the highest,
>> Glory to God and Jesus too,
> For all these souls now safe.

"The white ladies and gentlemen gathered round him," said Harriet, "till I couldn't see Joe for the crowd, only I heard his voice singing, 'Glory to God and Jesus too,' louder than ever." A sweet young lady reached over her fine cambric handkerchief to him, and as Joe wiped the great tears off his face, he said, "Tank de Lord! dere's only one more journey for me now, and dat's to Hebben!" As we bid farewell to Joe here, I may as well say that Harriet saw him several times after that, a happy and industrious freeman in Canada.[4]

He was tried twice for assisting in the escape of fugitive slaves, and was fined so heavily that everything he possessed was taken from him and sold to pay the fine. At the age of sixty he was left without a penny, but he went bravely to work, and in some measure regained his fortune; all the time aiding, in every way possible, all stray fugitives who applied to him for help.

Again he was arrested, tried, and heavily fined, and as the Judge of the United States Court pronounced the sentence, he said, in a solemn manner: "Garrett, let this be a lesson to you, not to interfere hereafter with the cause of justice, by helping off runaway negroes.

The old man, who had stood to receive his sentence, here raised his head, and fixing his eyes on "the Court," he said:

"Judge — thee hasn't left me a dollar, but I wish to say to thee, and to all in this court room, that if anyone knows of a fugitive who wants a shelter, and a friend, *send him to Thomas Garrett*, and he will befriend him!"

Not Luther before the Council at Worms was grander than this brave old man in his unswerving adherence to principle. In those days that tried men's souls there were many men like this old Quaker, and many women too, who would have gone cheerfully to the fire and the stake, for the cause of suffering humanity; men and women *these* "of whom the world was not worthy."

On one of her journeys to the North, as she was piloting a company of refugees, Harriet came, just as morning broke, to a town, where a colored man had lived whose house had been one of her stations of the under-ground, or unseen railroad. They reached the house, and leaving her party huddled together in the middle of the street, in a pouring rain, Harriet went to the door, and gave the peculiar rap which was her customary signal to her friends. There was not the usual ready response, and she was obliged to repeat the signal several times. At length a window was raised, and the head of a *white man* appeared, with the gruff question, "Who are you?" and "What do you want?" Harriet asked after her friend, and was told that he had been obliged to leave for "harboring niggers."

Here was an unforeseen trouble; day was breaking, and daylight was the enemy of the hunted and flying fugitives. Their faithful leader stood one moment in the street, and in that moment she had flashed a message quicker than that of the telegraph to her unseen Protector, and the answer came as quickly; in a suggestion to her of an almost forgotten place of refuge. Outside of the town there was a little island in a swamp, where the grass grew tall and rank, and where no human being could be suspected of seeking a hiding place. To this spot she conducted her party; she waded the swamp, carrying in a basket two well-drugged babies (these were a pair of little twins, whom I have since seen well grown young women), and the rest of the company following. She ordered them to lie down in the tall, wet grass, and here she prayed again, and waited for deliverance. The poor creatures were all cold, and wet, and hungry, and Harriet did not dare to leave them to get supplies; for no doubt the man at whose house she had knocked, had given the alarm in the town; and officers might be on the watch for them. They were truly in a wretched condition, but Harriet's faith never wavered, her silent prayer still ascended, and she confidently expected help from some quarter or other.

It was after dusk when a man came slowly walking along the solid pathway on the edge of the swamp. He was clad in the garb of a Quaker; and proved to be a "friend" in need and indeed; he seemed to be talking to himself, but ears quickened by sharp practice caught the words he was saying:

"My wagon stands in the barn-yard of the next farm across the way. The horse is in the stable; the harness hangs on a nail." And the man was gone. Night fell, and Harriet stole forth to the place designated. Not only a wagon, but a wagon well provisioned stood in the yard; and before many minutes the party were rescued from their wretched position, and were on their way rejoicing, to the next town. Here dwelt a Quaker whom Harriet knew, and he readily took charge of the horse and wagon, and no doubt returned them to their owner. How the good man who thus came to their rescue had received any intimation of their being in the neighborhood Harriet never knew. But these sudden deliverances never seemed to strike her as at all strange or mysterious; her prayer was the prayer of faith, and she *expected* an answer.

At one time, as she was on her way South for a party of slaves, she was stopped not far from the southern shore of the Chesapeake Bay, by a young woman, who had been for some days in hiding, and was anxiously watching for "Moses," who was soon expected to pass that way.

This girl was a young and pretty Mulatto, named Tilly, she had been lady's maid and dress-maker, for her Mistress. She was engaged to a young man from another plantation, but he had joined one of Harriet's parties, and gone North. Tilly was to have gone also at that time, but had found it impossible to get away. Now she had learned that it was her Master's intention to give her to a Negro of his own for his wife; and in fear and desperation, she made a strike for freedom. Friends had concealed her, and all had been on the watch for Moses.

The distress and excitement of the poor creature was so great, and she begged and implored in such agonized tones that Harriet would just see her safe to Baltimore, where she knew of friends who would harbor her, and help her on her way, that Harriet determined to turn about, and endeavor to take the poor girl thus far on her Northward journey.

They reached the shore of Chesapeake Bay too late to leave that night, and were obliged to hide for a night and day in the loft of an old out-house, where every sound caused poor Tilly to tremble as if she had an ague fit. When the time for the boat to leave arrived, a sad disappointment awaited them. The boat on which they had expected to leave was disabled, and another boat was to take its place. At that time, according to the law of Slavery, no Negro could leave his Master's land, or travel anywhere, without a pass, properly signed by his owner. Of course this poor fugitive had no pass; and Harriet's passes were her own wits; but among her many friends, there was one who seemed to have influence with the clerk of the boat, on which she expected to take passage; and she was the bearer of a note requesting, or commanding him to take these two women to the end of his route, asking no questions.

Now here was an unforeseen difficulty; the boat was not going; the clerk was not there; all on the other boat were strangers. But forward they must go, trusting in Providence. As they walked down to the boat, a gang of lazy white men standing together, began to make comments on their appearance.

"Too many likely looking Niggers traveling North, about these days." "Wonder if these wenches have got a pass." "Where you going, you two?" Tilly trembled and cowered, and clung to her protector, but Harriet put on a bold front, and holding the note given her by her friend in her hand, and supporting her terrified charge, she walked by the men, taking no notice of their insults.

They joined the stream of people going up to get their tickets, but when Harriet asked for hers, the clerk eyed her suspiciously, and said: "You just stand aside, you two; I'll attend to your case bye and bye."

Harriet led the young girl to the bow of the boat, where they were alone, and here, having no other help, she, as was her custom, addressed herself to the Lord. Kneeling on the seat, and supporting her head on her hands, and fixing her eyes on the waters of the bay, she groaned:

"Oh, Lord! You've been wid me in six troubles, *don't* desert me in the seventh!"

"Moses! Moses!" cried Tilly, pulling her by the sleeve. "Do go and see if you can't get tickets now."

"Oh, Lord! You've been wid me in six troubles, *don't* desert me in the seventh."

And so Harriet's story goes on in her peculiarly graphic manner, till at length in terror Tilly exclaimed:

"Oh, Moses! the man is coming. What shall we do?"

"Oh, Lord, you've been wid me in six troubles!"

Here the clerk touched her on the shoulder, and Tilly thought their time had come, but all he said was:

"You can come now and get your tickets," and their troubles were over.

What changed this man from his former suspicious and antagonistic aspect, Harriet never knew. Of course she said it was "de Lord," but as to the agency he used, she never troubled herself to inquire. She *expected* deliverance when she prayed, unless the Lord had ordered otherwise, and in that case she was perfectly willing to accept the Divine decree.

When surprise was expressed at her courage and daring, or at her unexpected deliverances, she would always reply: "Don't, I tell you, Missus, 'twan't *me*, 'twas *de Lord*! Jes' so long as he wanted to use me, he would take keer of me, an' when he didn't want me no longer, I was ready to go; I always tole him, I'm gwine to hole stiddy on to you, an' you've got to see me trou."

There came a time when Harriet, who had already brought away as many of her family as she could reach, besides all others who would trust themselves to her care, became much troubled in "spirit" about three of her brothers, having had an intimation of some kind that danger was impending over them. With her usual wonderful cunning, she employed a friend to write a letter for her to a man named Jacob Jackson, who lived near the plantation where these brothers were at that time the hired slaves.

Jacob Jackson was a free negro, who could both read and write, and who was under suspicion just then of having a hand in the disappearance of colored "property." It was necessary, therefore, to exercise great caution in writing to him, on his own account as well as that of the writer, and those whom she wished to aid. Jacob had an adopted son, William Henry Jackson, also free, who had come North. Harriet determined to sign her letter with William Henry's name, feeling sure that Jacob would be clever enough to understand by her peculiar phraseology, the meaning she intended to convey.

Therefore, after speaking of indifferent matters, the letter went on: "Read my letter to the old folks, and give my love to them, and tell my brothers to be always *watching unto prayer*, and when *the good old ship of Zion comes along, to be ready to step on board*." This letter was signed "William Henry Jackson."

Jacob was not allowed to have his letters in those days, until the self-elected inspectors of correspondence had had the perusal of them, and consulted over their secret meaning. These wise-acres therefore assembled, wiped their glasses carefully, put them on, and proceeded to examine this suspicious document. What it meant they could not imagine. William Henry Jackson had no parents, or brothers, and the letter was incomprehensible. Study as they might, no light dawned upon them, but their suspicions became stronger, and they were sure the letter meant mischief.

White genius having exhausted itself, black genius was brought into requisition. Jacob was sent for, and the letter was placed in his hands. He read between the lines, and comprehended the hidden meaning at once. "Moses" had dictated this letter, and Moses was coming. The brothers must be on the watch, and ready to join her at a moment's warning. But Moses must hurry, for the word had gone forth that the brothers were to be sent South, and the chain-gang was being collected.

Jacob read the letter slowly, threw it down, and said: "Dat letter can't be meant for me no how; I can't make head or tail of it." And he walked off and took immediate measures to let Harriet's brothers know that she was on the way, and they must be ready at the given signal to start for the North.

It was the day before Christmas when Harriet arrived, and the brothers were to have started on the day after Christmas for the South. They started on Christmas-day, but with their faces turned in another direction, and instead of the chain-gang and the whip, they had the North Star for their guide, and the Moses of her people for their leader.

As usual, this mysterious woman appeared suddenly, and word was conveyed to the brothers that they were to be at Old Ben's cabin on Saturday night, ready to start. "Old Ben" was their father, and as the parents were not of much use now, Harriet was pretty certain that they would not be sent away, and so she left them till she had rescued the younger and more valuable members of the family.

Quite a number had assembled at the cabin when the hour came for starting, but one brother was missing. Something had detained John; but when the time for starting had struck, Harriet's word was "forward," and she "nebber waited for no one."

Poor John was ready to start from his cabin in the negro quarter when his wife was taken ill, and in an hour or two another little heir to the blessings of slavery had come into the world.

John must go off for a "Granny," and being a faithful, affectionate creature, he could not leave his wife under the present circumstances.

After the birth of the child he determined to start. The North and freedom, or the South and life-long slavery, were the alternatives before him; and this was his last chance. If he once reached the North, he hoped with the help of Moses to bring his wife and children there.

Again and again he tried to start out of the door, but a watchful eye was on him, and he was always arrested by the question, "Where you gwine, John?" His wife had not been informed of the danger hanging over his head, but she knew he was uneasy, and she feared he was meditating a plan of escape. John told her he was going to try to get hired out on Christmas to another man, as that was the day on which such changes were made.

He left the house but stood near the window listening. He heard his wife sobbing and moaning, and not being able to endure it he went back to her. "Oh, John!" she cried, "you's gwine to lebe me! I know it! but wherebber you go, John, don't forgit me an' de little children."

John assured her that wherever he went she should come. He might not come for her, but he would send Moses, and then he hurried away. He had many miles to walk to his old father's cabin, where he knew the others would be waiting for him, and at daybreak he overtook them in the "fodder house," not far from the home of the old people.

At that time Harriet had not seen her mother for six years, but she did not dare to let her know that four of her children were so near her on their way to the North, for she would have raised such an uproar in her efforts to detain them, that the whole neighborhood would have been aroused.

The poor old woman had been expecting her sons to spend Christmas with her as usual. She had been hard at work in preparation for their arrival. The fatted pig had been killed, and had been converted into every form possible to the flesh of swine; pork, bacon and sausages were ready, but the boys did not come, and there she sat watching and waiting.

In the night when Harriet with two of her brothers, and two other fugitives who had joined them arrived at the "fodder house," they were exhausted and well-nigh famished. They sent the two strange men up to the cabin to try to rouse "Old Ben," but not to let their mother know that her children were so near her.

The men succeeded in rousing Old Ben, who came out quietly, and as soon as he heard their story, went back into the house, gathered together a quantity of provisions, and came down to the fodder house. He placed the provisions inside the door, saying a few words of welcome to his children, but taking care *not to see them*. "I know what'll come of dis," he said, "an' I ain't gwine to see my chillen, no how." The close espionage under which these poor creatures dwelt, engendered in them a cunning and artifice, which to them seemed only a fair and right attempt on their part, to cope with power and cruelty constantly in force against them.

Up among the ears of corn lay the old man's children, and one of them he had not seen for six years. It rained in torrents all that Sunday, and there they lay among the corn, for they could not start till night. At about daybreak John had joined them. There were wide chinks in the boards of the fodder house, and through these they could see the cabin of the old folks, now quite alone in their old age. All day long, every few minutes, they would see the old woman come out, and shading her eyes with her hand, take a long look down the road to see if "de boys" were coming, and then with a sad and disappointed air she would turn back into the cabin, and they could almost hear her sigh as she did so.

What had become of the boys? Had they been sold off down South? Had they tried to escape and been retaken? Would she never see them or hear of them more?

I have often heard it said by Southern people that "niggers had no feeling; they did not care when their children were taken from them." I have seen enough of them to know that their love for their offspring is quite equal to that of the "superior race," and it is enough to hear the tale of Harriet's endurance and self-sacrifice to rescue her brothers and sisters, to convince one that a heart, truer and more loving than that of many a white woman, dwelt in her bosom. I am quite willing to acknowledge that she was almost an anomaly among her people, but I have known many of her family, and so far as I can judge they all seem to be peculiarly intelligent, upright and religious people, and to have a strong feeling of family affection. There may be many among the colored race like them; certainly all should not be judged by the idle, miserable darkies who have swarmed about Washington and other cities since the War.

Two or three times while the group of fugitives were concealed in this loft of the fodder house, the old man came down and pushed food inside the door, and after nightfall he came again to accompany his children as far as he dared, upon their journey. When he reached the fodder house, he tied a handkerchief tight about his eyes, and one of his sons taking him by one arm, and Harriet taking him by the other, they went on their way talking in low tones together, asking and answering questions as to relatives and friends.

The time of parting came, and they bade him farewell, and left him standing in the middle of the road. When he could no longer hear their footsteps he turned back, and taking the handkerchief from his eyes, he hastened home.

But before Harriet and her brothers left, they had gone up to the cabin during the evening to take a silent farewell of the poor old mother. Through the little window of the cabin they saw her sitting by the fire, her head on her hand, rocking back and forth, as was her way when she was in great trouble; praying, no doubt, and wondering what had become of her children, and what new evil had befallen them.

With streaming eyes, they watched her for ten or fifteen minutes; but time was precious, and they must reach their next under-ground station before daylight, and so they turned sadly away.

When Christmas was over, and the men had not returned, there began to be no small stir in the plantation from which they had escaped. The first place to search, of course, was the home of the old people. At the "Big House" nothing had been seen of them. The master said "they had generally come up there to see the house servants, when they came for Christmas, but this time they hadn't been round at all. Better go down to Old Ben's, and ask him."

They went to Old Ben's. No one was at home but "Old Kit," the mother. She said "not one of 'em came dis Christmas. She was looking for 'em all day, an' her heart was mos' broke about 'em."

Old Ben was found and questioned about his sons. Old Ben said, "He hadn't *seen one* of 'em dis Christmas." With all his deep religious feeling, Old Ben thought that in such a case as this, it was enough for him to keep to the *letter*, and let the man hunters find his sons if they could. Old Ben knew the Old Testament stories well. Perhaps he thought of Rahab who hid the spies, and received a commendation for it. Perhaps of Jacob and Abraham, and some of their rather questionable proceedings. He knew the New Testament also, but I think perhaps he thought the kind and loving Saviour would have said to him, "Neither do I condemn thee." I doubt if he had read Mrs. Opie, and I wonder what judgment that excellent woman would have given in a case like this.

These poor fugitives, hunted like partridges upon the mountains, or like the timid fox by the eager sportsman, were obliged in self-defense to meet cunning with cunning, and to borrow from the birds and animals their mode of eluding their pursuers by any device which in the exigency of the case might present itself to them. They had a creed of their own, and a code of morals which we dare not criticise till we find our own lives and those of our dear ones similarly imperiled.

One of Harriet's other brothers had long been attached to a pretty mulatto girl named Catherine, who was owned by another master; but this man had other views for her, and would not let her marry William Henry. On one of Harriet's journeys this brother had made up his mind to make one of her next party to the North, and that Catherine should go also. He went to a tailor's and bought a new suit of clothes for a small person, and concealed them inside the fence of the garden of Catherine's master. This garden ran down to the bank of a little stream, and Catherine had been notified where to find the clothes. When the time came to get ready,

Catherine boldly walked down to the foot of the garden, took up the bundle, and hiding under the bank, she put on the man's garments and sent her own floating down the stream.

She was soon missed, and all the girls in the house were set to looking for Catherine. Presently they saw coming up from the river a well-dressed little darkey boy, and they all ceased looking for Catherine, and stared at him. He walked directly by them, round the house, and out of the gate, without the slightest suspicion being excited as to who he was. In a few weeks from that time, this party were all safe in Canada.

William Henry died in Canada, but I have seen and talked with Catherine at Harriet's house.

I am not quite certain which company it was that was under her guidance on their Northward way, but at one time when a number of men were following her, she received one of her sudden intimations that danger was ahead. "Chillen," she said, "we must stop here and cross dis ribber." They were on the bank of a stream of some width, and apparently a deep and rapid one. The men were afraid to cross; there was no bridge and no boat; but like her great pattern, she went forward into the waters, and the men not knowing what else to do, followed, but with fear and trembling. The stream did not divide to make a way for them to cross over, but to her was literally fulfilled the promise:

> "When through the deep waters I cause thee to go,
>   The rivers of sorrow shall not overflow."

"For," said she, "Missus, de water never came above my chin; when we thought surely we were all going under, it became shallower and shallower, and we came out safe on the odder side." Then there was another stream to cross, which was also passed in safety. They found afterward that a few rods ahead of them the advertisement of these escaping fugitives was posted up, and the officers, forewarned of their coming, were waiting for them. But though the Lord thus marvelously protected her from capture, she did not always escape the consequences of exposure like this. It was in March that this passage of the streams was effected, and the weather was raw and cold; Harriet traveled a long distance in her wet clothing, and was afterward very ill for a long time with a very severe cold. I have often heard her tell this story; but some of the incidents, particularly that of her illness, were not mentioned by herself, but were written me by friend Garrett.

I hardly know how to approach the subject of the spiritual experiences of my sable heroine. They seem so to enter into the realm of the supernatural, that I can hardly wonder that those who never knew her are ready to throw discredit upon the story. Ridicule has been cast upon the whole tale of her adventures by the advocates of human slavery; and perhaps by those who would tell with awe-struck countenance some tale of ghostly visitation, or spiritual manifestation, at a dimly lighted *"seance."*

Had I not known so well her deeply religious character, and her conscientious veracity, and had I not since the war, and when she was an inmate of my own house, seen such remarkable instances of what seemed to be her direct intercourse with heaven, I should not dare to risk my own character for veracity by making these things public in this manner.

But when I add that I have the strongest testimonials to her character for integrity from William H. Seward, Gerritt Smith, Wendell Phillips, Fred. Douglass, and my brother, Prof. S.M. Hopkins, who has known her for many years, I do not fear to brave the incredulity of any reader.

Governor Seward wrote of her:

"I have known Harriet long, and a nobler, higher spirit, or a truer, seldom dwells in human form."

Gerritt Smith, the distinguished philanthropist, was so kind as to write me expressing his gratification that I had undertaken this work, and added:

"I have often listened to Harriet with delight on her visits to my family, and I am convinced that she is not only truthful, but that she has a rare discernment, and a deep and sublime philanthropy."

Wendell Phillips wrote me, mentioning that in Boston, Harriet earned the confidence and admiration of all those who were working for freedom; and speaking of her labors during the war, he added: "In my opinion there are few captains, perhaps few colonels, who have done more for the loyal cause since the war began, and few men who did more before that time, for the colored race, than our fearless and sagacious friend."

Many other letters I received; from Mr. Sanborn, Secretary of the Massachusetts Board of Charities, from Fred. Douglass, from Rev. Henry Fowler, and from Union officers at the South during the war, all speaking in the highest praise and admiration of the character and labors of my black heroine.

Many of her passes also were sent me; in which she is spoken of as "Moses," for by that name she was universally known. For the story of her heroic deeds had gone before her, and the testimony of all who knew her accorded with the words of Mr. Seward:

"The cause of freedom owes her much; the country owes her much." And yet the country was not willing to pay her anything. Mr. Seward's efforts, seconded by other distinguished men, to get a pension for her, were sneered at in Congress as absurd and quixotic, and the effort failed.

Secretary Seward, from whom Harriet purchased her little place near Auburn, died. The place had been mortgaged when this noble woman left her home, and threw herself into the work needed for the Union cause; the mortgage was to be foreclosed. The old parents, then nearly approaching their centennial year, were to be turned out to die in a poor-house, when the sudden determination was taken to send out a little sketch of her life to the benevolent public, in the hope of redeeming the little home. This object, through the kindness of friends, was accomplished. The old people died in Harriet's own home, breathing blessings upon her for her devotion to them.

Now another necessity has arisen, and our sable friend, who never has been known to beg for herself, asks once more for help in accomplishing a favorite project for the good of her people. This, as she says, is "her last work, and she only prays de Lord to let her live till it is well started, and den she is ready to go." This work is the building of a hospital for old and disabled colored people; and in this she has already had the sympathy and aid of the good people of Auburn; the mayor and his noble wife having given her great assistance in the meetings she has held in aid of this object. It is partly to aid her in this work, on which she has so set her heart, that this story of her life and labors is being re-written.

At one time, when she felt called upon to go down for some company of slaves, she was, as she knew, watched for everywhere (for there had been an excited meeting of slave-holders, and they were determined to catch her, dead or alive), her friends gathered round her, imploring her not to go on in the face of danger and death, for they were sure she would never be allowed to return. And this was her answer:

"Now look yer! John saw de City, didn't he?" "Yes, John saw de City." "Well, what did he see? He saw twelve gates, didn't he? Three of dose gates was on de north; three of 'em was on de east; an' three of 'em was on de west; but dere was three more, an' dem was on de *south*; an' I reckon, if dey kill me down dere, I'll git into one of dem gates, don't you?"

Whether Harriet's ideas of the geographical bearings of the gates of the Celestial City as seen in the apocalyptic vision, were correct or not, we cannot doubt that she was right in the deduction her faith drew from them; and that somewhere, whether North, East, South, or West, to our dim vision, there is a gate that will be opened for our good Harriet, where the welcome will be given, "Come in, thou blessed of my Father."

It is a peculiarity of Harriet, that she had seldom been known to intimate a wish that anything should be given to herself; but when her people are in need, no scruples of delicacy stand in the way of her petitions, nay, almost her *demands* for help.

When, after rescuing so many others, and all of her brothers and sisters that could be reached, with their children, she received an intimation in some mysterious or supernatural way, that the old people were in trouble and needed her, she asked the Lord where she should go for the money to enable her to go for them. She was in some way, as she supposed, directed to the office of a certain gentleman, a friend of the slaves, in New York. When she left the house of the friends with whom she was staying, she said: "I'm gwine to Mr. — — —'s office, an' I ain't gwine to lebe dere, an' I ain't gwine to eat or drink, till I get money enough to take me down after de ole people."

She went into this gentleman's office.

"How do you do, Harriet? What do you want?" was the first greeting.

"I want some money, sir."

"*You do*! How much do you want?"

"I want twenty dollars, sir!"

"*Twenty dollars*! Who told you to come here for twenty dollars!"

"De Lord tole me, sir."

"He did; well I guess the Lord's mistaken this time."

"No, sir; de Lord's nebber mistaken! Anyhow I'm gwine to sit here till I get it."

So she sat down and went to sleep. All the morning, and all the afternoon, she sat there still; sometimes sleeping, sometimes rousing up, often finding the office full of gentlemen; sometimes finding herself alone. Many fugitives were passing through New York at this time, and those who came in supposed her to be one of them, tired out, and resting. Sometimes she would be roused up with the words:

"Come, Harriet! You had better go; there's no money for you here."

"No, sir; I'm not gwine to stir from here till I git my twenty dollars!"

She does not know all that happened, for deep sleep fell upon her; probably one of the turns of somnolency to which she has always been subject; but without doubt her story was whispered from one to another, and as her name and exploits were well known to many persons, the sympathies of some of those visitors to the office were aroused; at all events she came to full consciousness, at last, to find herself the happy possessor of *sixty dollars*, the contribution of these strangers. She went on her way rejoicing to bring her old parents from the land of bondage.

When she reached their home, she found that her old father was to be tried the next Monday for helping off slaves. And so, as she says in her forcible language, "I just removed my father's trial to a higher court, and brought him off to Canada."

The manner of their escape is detailed in the following letter from friend Garrett:

WILMINGTON, 6th Mo., 1868.

MY FRIEND: Thy favor of the 12th reached me yesterday, requesting such reminiscences as I could give respecting the remarkable labors of Harriet Tubman, in aiding her colored friends from bondage. I may begin by saying, living as I have in a slave State, and the laws being very severe where any proof could be made of any one aiding slaves on their way to freedom, I have not felt at liberty to keep any written word of Harriet's or my own labors, except in numbering those whom I have aided. For that reason I cannot furnish so interesting an account of Harriet's labors as I otherwise could, and now would be glad to do; for in truth I never met with any person, of any color, who had more confidence in the voice of God, as spoken direct to her soul. She has frequently told me that she talked with God, and he talked with her every day of her life, and she has declared to me that she felt no more fear of being arrested by her former master, or any other person, when in his immediate neighborhood, than she did in the State of New York, or Canada, for she said she never ventured only where God sent her, and her faith in the Supreme Power truly was great.

I have now been confined to my room with indisposition more than four weeks, and cannot sit to write much; but I feel so much interested in Harriet, that I will try to give some of the most remarkable incidents that now present themselves to my mind. The date of the commencement of her labors, I cannot certainly give; but I think it must have been about 1845; from that time till 1860, I think she must have brought from the neighborhood where she had been held as a slave, from 60 to 80 persons,[5] from Maryland, some 80 miles from here. No slave who placed himself under her care, was ever arrested that I have heard of; she mostly had her regular stopping places on her route; but in one instance, when she had several stout men with her, some 30 miles below here, she said that God told her to stop, which she did; and then asked him what she must do. He told her to leave the road, and turn to the left; she obeyed, and soon came to a small stream of tide water; there was no boat, no bridge; she again inquired of her Guide what she was to do. She was told to go through. It was cold, in the month of March; but having confidence in her Guide, she went in; the water came up to her armpits; the men refused to follow till they saw her safe on the opposite shore. They then followed, and, if I mistake not, she had soon to wade a second stream; soon after which she came to a cabin of colored people, who took them all in, put them to bed, and dried their clothes, ready to proceed next night on their journey. Harriet had run out of money, and gave them some of her underclothing to pay for their kindness. When she called on me two days after, she was so hoarse she could hardly speak, and was also suffering with violent toothache. The strange part of the story we found to be, that the masters of these men had put up the previous day, at the railroad station near where she left, an advertisement for them, offering a large reward for their apprehension; but they made a safe exit. She at one time brought as many as seven or eight, several of whom were women and children. She was well known here in Chester County and Philadelphia, and respected by all true abolitionists. I had been in the habit of furnishing her and those who accompanied her, as she returned from her acts of mercy, with new shoes; and on one occasion when I had not seen her for three months, she came into my store. I said, "Harriet, I am glad to see thee! I suppose thee wants a pair of new shoes." Her reply was, "I want more than that." I, in jest, said, "I have always been liberal with thee, and wish to be; but I am not rich, and cannot afford to give much." Her reply was: "God tells me you have money for me." I asked her "if God never deceived her?" She said, "No!" "Well! how much does thee want?" After studying a moment, she said: "About twenty-three dollars." I then gave her twenty-four dollars and some odd cents, the net proceeds of five pounds sterling, received through Eliza Wigham, of Scotland, for her. I had given some accounts of Harriet's labor to the Anti-Slavery Society of Edinburgh, of which Eliza Wigham was Secretary. On the reading of my letter, a gentleman present said he would send Harriet four pounds if he knew of any way to get it to her. Eliza Wigham offered to forward it to me for her, and that was the first money ever received by me for her. Some twelve months after, she called on me again, and said that God told her I had some money for her, but not so much as before. I had, a few days previous, received the net proceeds of one pound ten shillings from Europe for her. To say the least there was something remarkable in these facts, whether clairvoyance, or the divine impression on her mind from the source of all power, I cannot tell; but certain it was she had a guide within herself other than the written word, for she never had any education. She brought away her aged parents in a singular manner. They started with an old horse, fitted out in primitive style with a *straw collar*, a pair of old chaise wheels, with a board on the axle to sit on, another board swung with ropes, fastened to the axle, to rest their feet on. She got her parents, who were both slaves belonging to different masters, on this rude vehicle to the railroad, put them in the cars, turned Jehu herself, and drove to town in a style that no human being ever did before or since; but she was happy at having arrived safe. Next day, I furnished her with money to take them all to Canada. I afterward sold their horse, and sent them the balance of the proceeds. I believe that Harriet succeeded in freeing all her relatives but one sister and her three children. Etc., etc. Thy friend,

THOS. GARRETT.

As I have before stated, with all Harriet's reluctance to ask for anything for herself, no matter how great her needs may be, no such scruples trouble her if any of her people are in need. She never hesitates to call upon her kind friends in Auburn and in other places for help when her people are in want. At one time, when some such emergency had arisen, she went to see her friend, Governor Seward, and boldly presented her case to him.

"Harriet," he said, "you have worked for others long enough. If you would ever ask anything for yourself, I would gladly give it to you, but I will not help you to rob yourself for others any longer."

In spite of this apparent roughness, we may be sure Harriet did not leave this noble man's house empty handed.

And here I am reminded of a touching little circumstance that occurred at the funeral of Secretary Seward.

The great man lay in his coffin. Friends, children, and admirers were gathered there. Everything that love and wealth could do had been done; around him were floral emblems of every possible shape and design, that human ingenuity could suggest, or money could purchase. Just before the coffin was to be closed, a woman black as night stole quietly in, and laying a wreath of field flowers *on his feet*, as quietly glided out again. This was the simple tribute of our sable friend, and her last token of love and gratitude to her kind benefactor. I think he would have said, "This woman hath done more than ye all."

While preparing this second edition of Harriet's story, I have been much pleased to find that that good man, Oliver Johnson, is still living and in New York City. And I have just returned from a very pleasant interview with him. He remembers Harriet with great pleasure, though he has not seen her for many years. He speaks, as all who knew her do, of his entire confidence in her truthfulness and in the perfect integrity of her character.

He remembered her coming into his office with Joe, as I have stated it, and said he wished he could recall to me other incidents connected with her. But during those years, there were such numbers of fugitive slaves coming into the Anti-Slavery Office, that he might not tell the incidents of any one group correctly. No records were kept, as that would be so unsafe for the poor creatures, and those who aided them. He said, "You know Harriet never spoke of anything she had done, as if it was at all remarkable, or as if it deserved any commendation, but I remember one day, when she came into the office there was a Boston lady there, a warm-hearted, impulsive woman, who was engaged heart and hand in the Anti-Slavery cause.

"Harriet was telling, in her simple way, the story of her last journey. A party of fugitives were to meet her in a wood, that she might conduct them North. For some unexplained reason they did not come. Night came on and with it a blinding snow storm and a raging wind. She protected herself behind a tree as well as she could, and remained all night alone exposed to the fury of the storm."

"'Why, Harriet!' said this lady, 'didn't you almost feel when you were lying alone, as if there was *no God?*' 'Oh, no! missus,' said Harriet, looking up in her child-like, simple way, 'I jest asked Jesus to take keer of me, an' He never let me git *frost-bitten* one bit.'"

In 1860 the first gun was fired from Fort Sumter; and this was the signal for a rush to arms at the North and the South, and the war of the rebellion was begun. Troops were hurried off from the North to the West and the South, and battles raged in every part of the Southern States. By land and by sea, and on the Southern rivers, the conflict raged, and thousands and thousands of brave men shed their blood for what was maintained by each side to be the true principle.

This war our brave heroine had expected, and its result, the emancipation of the slaves. Three years before, while staying with the Rev. Henry Highland Garnet in New York, a vision came to her in the night of the emancipation of her people. Whether a dream, or one of those glimpses into the future, which sometimes seem to have been granted to her, no one can say, but the effect upon her was very remarkable.

She rose singing, "*My people are free!*" "*My people are free!*" She came down to breakfast singing the words in a sort of ecstasy. She could not eat. The dream or vision filled her whole soul, and physical needs were forgotten.

Mr. Garnet said to her:

"Oh, Harriet! Harriet! You've come to torment us before the time; do cease this noise! My grandchildren may see the day of the emancipation of our people, but you and I will never see it."

"I tell you, sir, you'll see it, and you'll see it soon. My people are free! My people are free."

When, three years later, President Lincoln's proclamation of emancipation was given forth, and there was a great jubilee among the friends of the slaves, Harriet was continually asked, "Why do you not join with the rest in their rejoicing!" "Oh," she answered, "I had *my* jubilee three years ago. I rejoiced all I could den; I can't rejoice no more."

In some of the Southern States, spies and scouts were needed to lead our armies into the interior. The ignorant and degraded slaves feared the "Yankee Buckra" more than they did their own masters, and after the proclamation of President Lincoln, giving freedom to the slaves, a person in whom these poor creatures could trust, was needed to assure them that these white Northern men were friends, and that they would be safe, trusting themselves in their hands.

In the early days of the war, Governor Andrew of Massachusetts, knowing well the brave and sagacious character of Harriet, sent for her, and asked her if she could go at a moment's notice, to act as spy and scout for our armies, and, if need be, to act as hospital nurse, in short, to be ready to give any required service to the Union cause.

There was much to be thought of; there were the old folks in the little home up in Auburn, there was the little farm of which she had taken the sole care; there were many dependents for whom she had provided by her daily toil. What was to become of them all if she deserted them? But the cause of the Union seemed to need her services, and after a few moments of reflection, she determined to leave all else, and go where it seemed that duty called her.

During those few years, the wants of the old people and of Harriet's other dependents were attended to by the kind people of Auburn. At that time, I often saw the old people, and wrote letters for them to officers at the South, asking from them tidings of Harriet. I received many letters in reply, all testifying to her faithfulness and bravery, and her untiring zeal for the welfare of our soldiers, black and white. She was often under fire from both armies; she led our forces through the jungle and the swamp, guided by an unseen hand. She gained the confidence of the slaves by her cheery words, and songs, and sacred hymns, and obtained from them much valuable information. She nursed our soldiers in the hospitals, and knew how, when they were dying by numbers of some malignant disease, with cunning skill to extract from roots and herbs, which grew near the source of the disease, the healing draught, which allayed the fever and restored numbers to health.

It is a shame to our government that such a valuable helper as this woman was not allowed pay or pension; but even was obliged to support herself during those days of incessant toil. Officers and men were paid. Indeed many enlisted from no patriotic motive, but because they were insured a support which they could not procure for themselves at home. But this woman sacrificed everything, and left her nearest and dearest, and risked her life hundreds of times for the cause of the Union, without one cent of recompense. She returned at last to her little home, to find it a scene of desolation. Her little place about to be sold to satisfy a mortgage, and herself without the means to redeem it.

Harriet was one of John Brown's "men." His brave and daring spirit found ready sympathy in her courageous heart; she sheltered him in her home in Canada, and helped him to plan his campaigns. I find in the life and letters of this remarkable man, written by Mr. F. B. Sanborn, occasional mention of Harriet, and her deep interest in Captain Brown's enterprises.

At one time he writes to his son from St. Catherine's, Canada:

"I came on here the day after you left Rochester. I am succeeding to all appearance beyond my expectations. Harriet Tubman *hooked on her whole team at once*. He (Harriet) is the most of a man naturally that I ever met with. There is abundant material here and of the right quality."

She suggested the 4th of July to him as the time to begin operations. And Mr. Sanborn adds: "It was about the 4th of July, as Harriet, the African sybil, had suggested, that Brown first showed himself in the counties of Washington and Jefferson, on opposite sides of the lordly Potomac."

I find among her papers, many of which are defaced by being carried about with her for years, portions of these letters addressed to myself, by persons at the South, and speaking of the valuable assistance Harriet was rendering our soldiers in the hospital, and our armies in the field. At this time her manner of life, as related by herself, was this:

"Well, missus, I'd go to de hospital, I would, early eb'ry mornin'. I'd get a big chunk of ice, I would, and put it in a basin, and fill it with water; den I'd take a sponge and begin. Fust man I'd come to, I'd thrash away de flies, and dey'd rise, dey would, like bees roun' a hive. Den I'd begin to bathe der wounds, an' by de time I'd bathed off three or four, de fire and heat would have melted de ice and made de water warm, an' it would be as red as clar blood. Den I'd go an' git more ice, I would, an' by de time I got to de nex' ones, de flies would be roun' de fust ones black an' thick as eber." In this way she worked, day after day, till late at night; then she went home to her little cabin, and made about fifty pies, a great quantity of ginger-bread, and two casks of root beer. These she would hire some contraband to sell for her through the camps, and thus she would provide her support for another day; for this woman never received pay or pension, and never drew for herself but twenty days' rations during the four years of her labors. At one time she was called away from Hilton Head, by one of our officers, to come to Fernandina, where the men were "dying off like sheep," from dysentery. Harriet had acquired quite a reputation for her skill in curing this disease, by a medicine which she prepared from roots which grew near the waters which gave the disease. Here she found thousands of sick soldiers and contrabands, and immediately gave up her time and attention to them. At another time, we find her nursing those who were down by hundreds with small-pox and malignant fevers. She had never had these diseases, but she seems to have no more fear of death in one form than another. "De Lord would take keer of her till her time came, an' den she was ready to go."

When our armies and gun-boats first appeared in any part of the South, many of the poor negroes were as much afraid of "de Yankee Buckra" as of their own masters. It was almost impossible to win their confidence, or to get information from them. But to Harriet they would tell anything; and so it became quite important that she should accompany expeditions going up the rivers, or into unexplored parts of the country, to control and get information from those whom they took with them as guides.

General Hunter asked her at one time if she would go with several gun-boats up the Combahee River, the object of the expedition being to take up the torpedoes placed by the rebels in the river, to destroy railroads and bridges, and to cut off supplies from the rebel troops. She said she would go if Colonel Montgomery was to be appointed commander of the expedition. Colonel Montgomery was one of John Brown's men, and was well known to Harriet. Accordingly, Colonel Montgomery was appointed to the command, and Harriet, with several men under her, the principal of whom was J. Plowden, whose pass I have, accompanied the expedition. Harriet describes in the most graphic manner the appearance of the plantations as they passed up the river; the frightened negroes leaving their work and taking to the woods, at sight of the gun-boats; then coming to peer out like startled deer, and scudding away like the wind at the sound of the steam-whistle. "Well," said one old negro, "Mas'r said de Yankees had horns and tails, but I nebber beliebed it till now." But the word was passed along by the mysterious telegraphic communication existing among these simple people, that these were "Lincoln's gun-boats come to set them free." In vain, then, the drivers used their whips in their efforts to hurry the poor creatures back to their quarters; they all turned and ran for the gun-boats. They came down every road, across every field, just as they had left their work and their cabins; women with children clinging around their necks, hanging to their dresses, running behind, all making at full speed for "Lincoln's gun-boats." Eight hundred poor wretches at one time crowded the banks, with their hands extended toward their deliverers, and they were all taken off upon the gun-boats, and carried down to Beaufort.

"I nebber see such a sight," said Harriet; "we laughed, an' laughed, an' laughed. Here you'd see a woman wid a pail on her head, rice a smokin' in it jus' as she'd taken it from de fire, young one hangin' on behind, one han' roun' her forehead to hold on, 'tother han' diggin' into de rice-pot, eatin' wid all its might; hold of her dress two or three more; down her back a bag wid a pig in it. One woman brought two pigs, a white one an' a black one; we took 'em all on board; named de white pig Beauregard, and de black pig Jeff Davis. Sometimes de women would come wid twins hangin' roun' der necks; 'pears like I nebber see so many twins in my life; bags on der shoulders, baskets on der heads, and young ones taggin' behin', all loaded; pigs squealin', chickens screamin', young ones squallin'." And so they came pouring down to the gun-boats. When they stood on the shore, and the small boats put out to take them off, they all wanted to get in at once. After the boats were crowded, they would hold on to them so that they could not leave the shore. The oarsmen would beat them on their hands, but they would not let go; they were afraid the gun-boats would go off and leave them, and all wanted to make sure of one of these arks of refuge. At length Colonel Montgomery shouted from the upper deck, above the clamor of appealing tones, "Moses, you'll have to give em a song." Then Harriet lifted up her voice, and sang:

> "Of all the whole creation in the East or in the West,
> The glorious Yankee nation is the greatest and the best.
> Come along! Come along! don't be alarmed,
> Uncle Sam is rich enough to give you all a farm."

At the end of every verse, the negroes in their enthusiasm would throw up their hands and shout "Glory," and the row-boats would take that opportunity to push off; and so at last they were all brought on board. The masters fled; houses and barns and railroad bridges were burned, tracks torn up, torpedoes destroyed, and the object of the expedition was fully accomplished.

This fearless woman was often sent into the rebel lines as a spy, and brought back valuable information as to the position of armies and batteries; she has been in battle when the shot was falling like hail, and the bodies of dead and wounded men were dropping around her like leaves in autumn; but the thought of fear never seems to have had place for a moment in her mind. She had her duty to perform, and she expected to be taken care of till it was done.

Would that, instead of taking them in this poor way at second-hand, my readers could hear this woman's graphic accounts of scenes she herself witnessed, could listen to her imitations of negro preachers in their own very peculiar dialect, her singing of camp-meeting hymns, her account of "experience meetings," her imitations of the dances, and the funeral ceremonies of these simple people. "Why, der language down dar in de far South is jus' as different from ours in Maryland as you can tink," said she. "Dey laughed when dey heard me talk, an' I could not understand dem, no how." She described a midnight funeral which she attended; for the slaves, never having been allowed to bury their dead in the day-time, continued the custom of night funerals from habit.

The corpse was laid upon the ground, and the people all sat round, the group being lighted up by pine torches.

The old negro preacher began by giving out a hymn, which was sung by all. "An' oh! I wish you could hear 'em sing, Missus," said Harriet. "Der voices is so sweet, and dey can sing eberyting we sing, an' den dey can sing a great many hymns dat we can't nebber catch at all."

The old preacher began his sermon by pointing to the dead man, who lay in a rude box on the ground before him.

"Shum? Ded-a-de-dah! Shum, David? Ded-a-de-dah! Now I want you all to flec' for moment. Who ob all dis congregation is gwine next to lie ded-e-de-dah? You can't go nowhere's, my frien's and bredren, but Deff 'll fin' you. You can't dig no hole so deep an' bury yourself dar, but God A'mighty's far-seein' eye'll fin' you, an' Deff 'll come arter you. You can't go into that big fort (pointing to Hilton Head), an' shut yourself up dar; dat fort dat Sesh Buckra said the debil couldn't take, but Deff 'll fin' you dar. All your frien's may forget you, but Deff 'll nebber forget you. Now, my bredren, prepare to lie ded-a-de-dah!"

This was the burden of a very long sermon, after which the whole congregation went round in a sort of solemn dance, called the "spiritual shuffle," shaking hands with each other, and calling each other by name as they sang:

"My sis'r Mary's boun' to go;
My sis'r Nanny's boun' to go;
My brudder Tony's boun' to go;
My brudder July's boun' to go."

This to the same tune, till every hand had been shaken by every one of the company. When they came to Harriet, who was a stranger, they sang:

Eberybody's boun' to go!

The body was then placed in a Government wagon, and by the light of the pine torches, the strange, dark procession moved along, singing a rude funeral hymn, till they reached the place of burial.

Harriet's account of her interview with an old negro she met at Hilton Head, is amusing and interesting. He said, "I'd been yere seventy-three years, workin' for my master widout even a dime wages. I'd worked rain-wet sun-dry. I'd worked wid my mouf full of dust, but could not stop to get a drink of water. I'd been whipped, an' starved, an' I was always prayin', 'Oh! Lord, come an' delibber us!' All dat time de birds had been flyin', an' de rabens had been cryin', and de fish had been swimmin' in de waters. One day I look up, an' I see a big cloud; it didn't come up like as de clouds come out far yonder, but it 'peared to be right ober head. Der was thunders out of dat, an' der was lightnin's. Den I looked down on de water, an' I see, 'peared to me a big house in de water, an' out of de big house came great big eggs, and de good eggs went on trou' de air, an' fell into de fort; an' de bad eggs burst before dey got dar. Den de Sesh Buckra begin to run, an' de neber stop running till de git to de swamp, an' de stick dar an' de die dar. Den I heard 'twas de Yankee ship⁶ firin' out de big eggs, an dey had come to set us free. Den I praise de Lord. He come an' put he little finger in de work, an de Sesh Buckra all go; and de birds stop flyin', and de rabens stop cryin', an' when I go to catch a fish to eat wid my rice, dey's no fish dar. De Lord A'mighty 'd come and frightened 'em all out of de waters. Oh! Praise de Lord! I'd prayed seventy-three years, an' now he's come an' we's all free."

The following account of the subject of this memoir is cut from the *Boston Commonwealth* of 1863, kindly sent the writer by Mr. Sanborn:

"It was said long ago that the true romance of America was not in the fortunes of the Indian, where Cooper sought it, nor in New England character, where Judd found it, nor in the social contrasts of Virginia planters, as Thackeray imagined, but in the story of the fugitive slaves. The observation is as true now as it was before War, with swift, gigantic hand, sketched the vast shadows, and dashed in the high lights in which romance loves to lurk and flash forth. But the stage is enlarged on which these dramas are played, the whole world now sit as spectators, and the desperation or the magnanimity of a poor black woman has power to shake the nation that so long was deaf to her cries. We write of one of these heroines, of whom our slave annals are full — a woman whose career is as extraordinary as the most famous of her sex can show.

"Araminta Ross, now known by her married name of Tubman, with her sounding Christian name changed to Harriet, is the grand-daughter of a slave imported from Africa, and has not a drop of white blood in her veins. Her parents were Benjamin Ross and Harriet Greene, both slaves, but married and faithful to each other. They still live in old age and poverty,⁷ but free, on a little property at Auburn, N.Y., which their daughter purchased for them from Mr. Seward, the Secretary of State. She was born, as near as she can remember, in 1820 or in 1821, in Dorchester County, on the Eastern shore of Maryland, and not far from the town of Cambridge. She had ten brothers and sisters, of whom three are now living, all at the North, and all rescued from slavery by Harriet, before the War. She went back just as the South was preparing to secede, to bring away a fourth, but before she could reach her, she was dead. Three years before, she had brought away her old father and mother, at great risk to herself.

"When Harriet was six years old, she was taken from her mother and carried ten miles to live with James Cook, whose wife was a weaver, to learn the trade of weaving. While still a mere child, Cook set her to watching his musk-rat traps, which compelled her to wade through the water. It happened that she was once sent when she was ill with the measles, and, taking cold from wading in the water in this condition, she grew very sick, and her mother persuaded her master to take her away from Cook's until she could get well.

"Another attempt was made to teach her weaving, but she would not learn, for she hated her mistress, and did not want to live at home, as she would have done as a weaver, for it was the custom then to weave the cloth for the family, or a part of it, in the house.

"Soon after she entered her teens she was hired out as a field hand, and it was while thus employed that she received a wound, which nearly proved fatal, from the effects of which she still suffers. In the fall of the year, the slaves there work in the evening, cleaning up wheat, husking corn, etc. On this occasion, one of the slaves of a farmer named Barrett, left his work, and went to the village store in the evening. The overseer followed him, and so did Harriet. When the slave was found, the overseer swore he should be whipped, and called on Harriet, among others, to help tie him. She refused, and as the man ran away, she placed herself in the door to stop pursuit. The overseer caught up a two-pound weight from the counter and threw it at the fugitive, but it fell short and struck Harriet a stunning blow on the head. It was long before she recovered from this, and it has left her subject to a sort of stupor or lethargy at times; coming upon her in the midst of conversation, or whatever she may be doing, and throwing her into a deep slumber, from which she will presently rouse herself, and go on with her conversation or work.

"After this she lived for five or six years with John Stewart, where at first she worked in the house, but afterward 'hired her time,' and Dr. Thompson, son of her master's guardian, 'stood for her,' that is, was her surety for the payment of what she owed. She employed the time thus hired in the rudest labors, — drove oxen, carted, plowed, and did all the work of a man, — sometimes earning money enough in a year, beyond what she paid her master, 'to buy a pair of steers,' worth forty dollars. The amount exacted of a woman for her time was fifty or sixty dollars — of a man, one hundred to one hundred and fifty dollars. Frequently Harriet worked for her father, who was a timber inspector, and superintended the cutting and hauling of great quantities of timber for the Baltimore ship-yards. Stewart, his temporary master, was a builder, and for the work of Ross used to receive as much as five dollars a day sometimes, he being a superior workman. While engaged with her father, she would cut wood, haul logs, etc. Her usual 'stint' was half a cord of wood in a day.

"Harriet was married somewhere about 1844, to a free colored man named John Tubman, but she had no children. For the last two years of slavery she lived with Dr. Thompson, before mentioned, her own master not being yet of age, and Dr. T.'s father being his guardian, as well as the owner of her own father. In 1849 the young man died, and the slaves were to be sold, though previously set free by an old will. Harriet resolved not to be sold, and so, with no knowledge of the North — having only heard of Pennsylvania and New Jersey — she walked away one night alone. She found a friend in a white lady, who knew her story and helped her on her way. After many adventures, she reached Philadelphia, where she found work and earned a small stock of money. With this money in her purse, she traveled back to Maryland for her husband, but she found him married to another woman, and no longer caring to live with her. This, however, was not until two years after her escape, for she does not seem to have reached her old home in the first two expeditions. In December, 1850, she had visited Baltimore and brought away her sister and two children, who had come up from Cambridge in a boat, under charge of her sister's husband, a free black. A few months after she had brought away her brother and two other men, but it was not till the fall of 1851, that she found her husband and learned of his infidelity. She did not give way to rage or grief, but collected a party of fugitives and brought them safely to Philadelphia. In December of the same year, she returned, and led out a party of eleven, among them her brother and his wife. With these she journeyed to Canada, and there spent the winter, for this was after the enforcement of Mason's Fugitive Slave Bill in Philadelphia and Boston, and there was no safety except 'under the paw of the British Lion,' as she quaintly said. But the first winter was terribly severe for these poor runaways. They earned their bread by chopping wood in the snows of a Canadian forest; they were frost-bitten, hungry, and naked. Harriet was their good angel. She kept house for her brother, and the poor creatures boarded with her. She worked for them, begged for them, prayed for them, with the strange familiarity of communion with God which seems natural to these people, and carried them by the help of God through the hard winter.

"In the spring she returned to the States, and as usual earned money by working in hotels and families as a cook. From Cape May, in the fall of 1852, she went back once more to Maryland, and brought away nine more fugitives.

"Up to this time she had expended chiefly her own money in these expeditions — money which she had earned by hard work in the drudgery of the kitchen. Never did any one more exactly fulfill the sense of George Herbert —

"'A servant with this clause
  Makes drudgery divine.'

"But it was not possible for such virtues long to remain hidden from the keen eyes of the Abolitionists. She became known to Thomas Garrett, the large-hearted Quaker of Wilmington, who has aided the escape of three thousand fugitives; she found warm friends in Philadelphia and New York, and wherever she went. These gave her money, which he never spent for her own use, but laid up for the help of her people, and especially for her journeys back to the 'land of Egypt,' as she called her old home. By reason of her frequent visits there, always carrying away some of the oppressed, she got among her people the name of 'Moses,' which it seems she still retains.

"Between 1852 and 1857, she made but two of these journeys, in consequence partly of the increased vigilance of the slave-holders, who had suffered so much by the loss of their property. A great reward was offered for her capture and she several times was on the point of being taken, but always escaped by her quick wit, or by 'warnings' from Heaven — for it is time to notice one singular trait in her character. She is the most shrewd and practical person in the world, yet she is a firm believer in omens, dreams, and warnings. She declares that before her escape from slavery, she used to dream of flying over fields and towns, and rivers and mountains, looking down upon them 'like a bird,' and reaching at last a great fence, or sometimes a river, over which she would try to fly, 'but it 'peared like I wouldn't hab de strength, and jes as I was sinkin' down, dere would be ladies all drest in white ober dere, and dey would put out dere arms and pull me 'cross.' There is nothing strange in this, perhaps, but she declares that when she came North she remembered these very places as those she had seen in her dreams, and many of the ladies who befriended her were those she had been helped by in her vision.

"Then she says she always knows when there is danger near her — she does not know how, exactly, but "pears like my heart go flutter, flutter, and den dey may say "Peace, Peace," as much as dey likes, *I know its gwine to be war!*' She is very firm on this point, and ascribes to this her great impunity, in spite of the lethargy before mentioned, which would seem likely to throw her into the hands of her enemies. She says she inherited this power, that her father could always predict the weather, and that he foretold the Mexican war.

"In 1857 she made her most venturesome journey, for she brought with her to the North her old parents, who were no longer able to walk such distances as she must go by night. Consequently she must hire a wagon for them, and it required all her ingenuity to get them through Maryland and Delaware safe. She accomplished it, however, and by the aid of her friends she brought them safe to Canada, where they spent the winter. Her account of their sufferings there — of her mother's complaining and her own philosophy about it — is a lesson of trust in

Providence better than many sermons. But she decided to bring them to a more comfortable place, and so she negotiated with Mr. Seward — then in the Senate — for a little patch of ground. To the credit of the Secretary of State it should be said, that he sold her the property on very favorable terms, and gave her some time for payment. To this house she removed her parents, and set herself to work to pay for the purchase. It was on this errand that she first visited Boston — we believe in the winter of 1858-59. She brought a few letters from her friends in New York, but she could herself neither read nor write, and she was obliged to trust to her wits that they were delivered to the right persons. One of them, as it happened, was to the present writer, who received it by another hand, and called to see her at her boarding-house. It was curious to see the caution with which she received her visitor until she felt assured that there was no mistake. One of her means of security was to carry with her the daguerreotypes of her friends, and show them to each new person. If they recognized the likeness, then it was all right.

"Pains were taken to secure her the attention to which her great services of humanity entitled her, and she left New England with a handsome sum of money toward the payment of her debt to Mr. Seward. Before she left, however, she had several interviews with Captain Brown, then in Boston. He is supposed to have communicated his plans to her, and to have been aided by her in obtaining recruits and money among her people. At any rate, he always spoke of her with the greatest respect, and declared that 'General Tubman,' as he styled her, was a better officer than most whom he had seen, and could command an army as successfully as she had led her small parties of fugitives.

"Her own veneration for Captain Brown has always been profound, and since his murder, has taken the form of a religion. She had often risked her own life for her people, and she thought nothing of that; but that a white man, and a man so noble and strong, should so take upon himself the burden of a despised race, she could not understand, and she took refuge from her perplexity in the mysteries of her fervid religion.

"Again, she laid great stress on a dream which she had just before she met Captain Brown in Canada. She thought she was in 'a wilderness sort of place, all full of rocks, and bushes,' when she saw a serpent raise its head among the rocks, and as it did so, it became the head of an old man with a long white beard, gazing at her, 'wishful like, jes as ef he war gwine to speak to me,' and then two other heads rose up beside him, younger than he, — and as she stood looking at them, and wondering what they could want with her, a great crowd of men rushed in and struck down the younger heads, and then the head of the old man, still looking at her so 'wishful.' This dream she had again and again, and could not interpret it; but when she met Captain Brown, shortly after, behold, he was the very image of the head she had seen. But still she could not make out what her dream signified, till the news came to her of the tragedy of Harper's Ferry, and then she knew the two other heads were his two sons. She was in New York at that time, and on the day of the affair at Harper's Ferry she felt her usual warning that something was wrong — she could not tell what. Finally she told her hostess that it must be Captain Brown who was in trouble, and that they should soon hear bad news from him. The next day's newspaper brought tidings of what had happened.

"Her last visit to Maryland was made after this, in December, 1860; and in spite of the agitated condition of the country, and the greater watchfulness of the slave-holders, she brought away seven fugitives, one of them an infant, which must be drugged with opium to keep it from crying on the way, and so revealing the hiding-place of the party."

In the spring of 1860, Harriet Tubman was requested by Mr. Gerrit Smith to go to Boston to attend a large Anti-Slavery meeting. On her way, she stopped at Troy to visit a cousin, and while there the colored people were one day startled with the intelligence that a fugitive slave, by the name of Charles Nalle, had been followed by his master (who was his younger brother, and not one grain whiter than he), and that he was already in the hands of the officers, and was to be taken back to the South. The instant Harriet heard the news, she started for the office of the United States Commissioner, scattering the tidings as she went. An excited crowd was gathered about the office, through which Harriet forced her way, and rushed up stairs to the door of the room where the fugitive was detained. A wagon was already waiting before the door to carry off the man, but the crowd was even then so great, and in such a state of excitement, that the officers did not dare to bring the man down. On the opposite side of the street stood the colored people, watching the window where they could see Harriet's sun-bonnet, and feeling assured that so long as she stood there, the fugitive was still in the office. Time passed on, and he did not appear. "They've taken him out another way, depend upon that," said some of the colored people. "No," replied others, "there stands 'Moses' yet, and as long as she is there, he is safe." Harriet, now seeing the necessity for a tremendous effort for his rescue, sent out some little boys to cry *fire*. The bells rang, the crowd increased, till the whole street was a dense mass of people. Again and again the officers came out to try and clear the stairs, and make a way to take their captive down; others were driven down, but Harriet stood her ground, her head bent and her arms folded. "Come, old woman, you must get out of this," said one of the officers; "I must have the way cleared; if you can't get down alone, some one will help you." Harriet, still putting on a greater appearance of decrepitude, twitched away from him, and kept her place. Offers were made to buy Charles from his master, who at first agreed to take twelve hundred dollars for him; but when this was subscribed, he immediately raised the price to fifteen hundred. The crowd grew more excited. A gentleman raised a window and called out, "Two hundred dollars for his rescue, but not one cent to his master!" This was responded to by a roar of satisfaction from the crowd below. At length the officers appeared, and announced to the crowd, that if they would open a lane to the wagon, they would promise to bring the man down the front way.

The lane was opened, and the man was brought out — a tall, handsome, intelligent *white* man, with his wrists manacled together, walking between the U.S. Marshal and another officer, and behind him his brother and his master, so like him that one could hardly be told from the other. The moment they appeared, Harriet roused from her stooping posture, threw up a window, and cried to her friends: "Here he comes — take him!" and then darted down the stairs like a wild-cat. She seized one officer and pulled him down, then another, and tore him away from the man; and keeping her arms about the slave, she cried to her friends: "Drag us out! Drag him to the river! Drown him! but don't let them have him!" They were knocked down together, and while down, she tore off her sun-bonnet and tied it on the head of the fugitive. When he rose, only his head could be seen, and amid the surging mass of people the slave was no longer recognized, while the master appeared like the slave. Again and again they were knocked down, the poor slave utterly helpless, with his manacled wrists, streaming with blood. Harriet's outer clothes were torn from her, and even her stout shoes were pulled from her feet, yet she never relinquished her hold of the man, till she had dragged him to the river, where he was tumbled into a boat, Harriet following in a ferry-boat to the other side. But the telegraph was ahead of them, and as soon as they landed he was seized and hurried from her sight. After a time, some school children came hurrying along, and to her anxious inquiries they answered, "He is up in that house, in the third story." Harriet rushed up to the place. Some men were attempting to make their way up the stairs. The officers were firing down, and two men were lying on the stairs, who had been shot. Over their bodies our heroine rushed, and with the help of others burst open the door of the room, and dragged out the fugitive, whom Harriet carried down stairs in her arms. A gentleman who was riding by with a fine horse, stopped to ask what the disturbance meant; and on hearing the story, his sympathies seemed to be thoroughly aroused; he sprang from his wagon, calling out, "That is a blood-horse, drive him till he drops." The poor man was hurried in; some of his friends jumped in after him, and drove at the most rapid rate to Schenectady.

This is the story Harriet told to the writer. By some persons it seemed too wonderful for belief, and an attempt was made to corroborate it. Rev. Henry Fowler, who was at the time at Saratoga, kindly volunteered to go to Troy and ascertain the facts. His report was, that he had had a long interview with Mr. Townsend, who acted during the trial as counsel for the slave, that he had given him a "rich narration," which he would write out the next week for this little book. But before he was to begin his generous labor, and while engaged in some kind efforts for the prisoners at Auburn, he was stricken down by the heat of the sun, and was for a long time debarred from labor.

This good man died not long after and the promised narration was never written, but a statement by Mr. Townsend was sent me, which I copy here:

Statements made by Martin I. Townsend, Esq., of Troy, who was counsel for the fugitive, Charles Nalle.

Nalle is an octoroon; his wife has the same infusion of Caucasian blood. She was the daughter of her master, and had, with her sister, been bred by him in his family, as his own child. When the father died, both of these daughters were married and had large families of children. Under the highly Christian national laws of "Old Virginny," these children were the slaves of their grandfather. The old man died, leaving a will, whereby he manumitted his daughters and their children, and provided for the purchase of the freedom of their husbands. The manumission of the children and grandchildren took effect; but the estate was insufficient to purchase the husbands of his daughters, and the fathers of his grandchildren. The manumitted, by another Christian, "conservative," and "national" provision of law, were forced to leave the State, while the slave husbands remained in slavery. Nalle, and his brother-in-law, were allowed for a while to visit their families outside Virginia about once a year, but were at length ordered to provide themselves with new wives, as they would be allowed to visit their former ones no more. It was after this that Nalle and his brother-in-law started for the land of freedom, guided by the steady light of the north star. Thank God, neither family now need fear any earthly master or the bay of the blood-hound dogging their fugitive steps.

Nalle returned to Troy with his family about July, 1860, and resided with them there for more than seven years. They are all now residents of the city of Washington, D.C. Nalle and his family are persons of refined manners, and of the highest respectability. Several of his children are red-haired, and a stranger would discover no trace of African blood in their complexions or features. It was the head of this family whom H.F. Averill proposed to doom to returnless exile and life-long slavery.

When Nalle was brought from Commissioner Beach's office into the street, Harriet Tubman, who had been standing with the excited crowd, rushed amongst the foremost to Nalle, and running one of her arms around his manacled arm, held on to him without ever loosening her hold through the more than half-hour's struggle to Judge Gould's office, and from Judge Gould's office to the dock, where Nalle's liberation was accomplished. In the *mêelée* she was repeatedly beaten over the head with policemen's clubs, but she never for a moment released her hold, but cheered Nalle and his friends with her voice, and struggled with the officers until they were literally worn out with their exertions, and Nalle was separated from them.

True, she had strong and earnest helpers in her struggle, some of whom had white faces as well as human hearts, and are now in Heaven. But she exposed herself to the fury of the sympathizers with slavery, without fear, and suffered their blows without flinching. Harriet crossed the river with the crowd, in the ferry-boat, and when the men who led the assault upon the door of Judge Stewart's office were stricken down, Harriet and a number of other colored women rushed over their bodies, brought Nalle out, and putting him in the first wagon passing, started him for the West.

A lively team, driven by a colored man, was immediately sent on to relieve the other, and Nalle was seen about Troy no more until he returned a free man by purchase from his master. Harriet also disappeared, and the crowd dispersed. How she came to be in Troy that day, is entirely unknown to our citizens; and where she hid herself after the rescue, is equally a mystery. But her struggle was in the sight of a thousand, perhaps of five thousand spectators.

On asking Harriet particularly, as to the age of her mother, she answered, "Well, I'll tell you, Missus. Twenty-three years ago, in Maryland, I paid a lawyer five dollars to look up the will of my mother's first master. He looked back sixty years, and said it was time to give up. I told him to go back furder. He went back sixty-five years, and there he found the will — giving the girl Ritty to his grand-daughter (Mary Patterson), to serve her and her offspring till she was forty-five years of age." This grand-daughter died soon after, unmarried; and as there was no provision for Ritty, in case of her death, she was actually emancipated at that time. But no one informed her of the fact, and she and her dear children remained in bondage till emancipated by the courage and determination of this heroic daughter and sister. The old woman must then, it seems, be ninety-eight years of age,[8] and the old man has probably numbered as many years. And yet these old people, living out beyond the toll-gate, on the South Street road, Auburn, come in every Sunday — more than a mile — to the Central Church. To be sure, deep slumbers settle down upon them as soon as they are seated, which continue undisturbed till the congregation is dismissed; but they have done their best, and who can doubt that they receive a blessing. Immediately after this they go to class-meeting at the Methodist Church. Then they wait for a third service, and after that start out home again.

Harriet supposes that the whole family were actually free, and were kept wrongfully in a state of slavery all those long years; but she simply states the fact, without any mourning or lamenting over the wrong and the misery of it all, accepting it as the will of God, and, therefore, not to be rebelled against.

This woman, of whom you have been reading, is now old and feeble, suffering from the effects of her life of unusual labor and hardship, as well as from repeated injuries; but she is still at work for her people. For many years, even long before the war, her little home has been the refuge of the hunted and the homeless, for whom she had provided; and I have seen as many as eight or ten dependents upon her care at one time living there.

It has always been a hospital, but she feels the need of a large one, and only prays to see this, "her last work," completed ere she goes hence.

Without claiming any of my dear old Harriet's prophetic vision, I seem to see a future day when the wrongs of earth will be righted, and justice, long delayed, will assert itself. I seem to see that our poor Harriet has passed within "one of dem gates," and has received the welcome, "Come, thou blessed of my Father; for I was hungry and you gave me meat, I was thirsty and you gave me drink, I was a stranger and you took me in, naked and you clothed me, sick and in prison and you visited me."

And when she asks, "Lord, when did I do all this?" He answers:

"Inasmuch as you did it unto one of the least of these, *my brethren*, you did it unto me."

And as she stands in her modest way just within the celestial gate, I seem to see a kind hand laid upon her dark head, and to hear a gentle voice saying in her ear, "Friend, come up higher!"

SOME ADDITIONAL INCIDENTS IN THE LIFE OF "HARRIET"

The story of this remarkable black woman has been attracting renewed interest of late, and I have often been asked to publish another edition of the book, and to add some interesting and amusing incidents which I have related to my friends.

Harriet is very old and feeble now; she does not know how old, but probably between eighty and ninety. Her years of toil and adventure have told upon her, and she may not last much longer. If she does, she will still need help which she would never ask for herself, but which this little book may give her; when she dies, it may aid in putting up a fitting monument to her memory, which should always be "kept green."

As time goes on, the horrors of the days of slavery are by many forgotten, and the children who have been born since the War of the Rebellion know of that fearful straggle, and of the causes that led to it, only as a tradition of long ago.

Even in the city where Harriet has so long lived her quiet and unobtrusive life, it is not an uncommon thing to meet a young person who has never even heard her name.

Those who know the principal facts of her eventful history may be interested to read these few added incidents, which she has related to me from time to time.

A year or two ago, as I was staying at the summer home of my brother, Professor Hopkins, on Owasco Lake, Harriet came up to see us; it was after lunch, and my brother ordered a table to be set for her on the broad shaded piazza and waited on her himself, bringing her cups of tea and other good things, as if it were a pleasure and an honor to serve her.

There is a quiet dignity about Harriet that makes her superior or indifferent to all surrounding circumstances; whether seated at the hospitable board of Gerrit Smith or any other white gentleman, as she often was, or sent to the kitchen, where the white domestics refused to eat with a "nigger," it was all the same to Harriet; she was never elated, or humiliated; she took everything as it came, making no comments or complaints.

And so she sat quietly eating her lunch, and talking with us. After the lunch was over, as we sat on the piazza waiting for the steamboat to take her back to Auburn, she said:

"I often think, Missus, of things I wish I had told you before you wrote de book. Now, as I come up on de boat I thought of one thing thet happened to me when I was very little.

"I was only seven years old when I was sent away to take car' of a baby. I was so little dat I had to sit down on de flo' and hev de baby put in my lap. An' dat baby was allus in my lap 'cept when it was asleep, or its mother was feedin' it.

"One mornin' after breakfast she had de baby, an' I stood by de table waitin' till I was to take it; just by me was a bowl of lumps of white sugar. My Missus got into a great quarrel wid her husband; she had an awful temper, an' she would scole an' storm, an' call him all sorts of names. Now you know, Missus, I never had nothing good; no sweet, no sugar, an' dat sugar, right by me, did look so nice, an' my Missus's back was turned to me while she was fightin' wid her husband, so I jes' put my fingers in de sugar bowl to take one lump, an' maybe she heard me, an' she turned an' saw me. De nex' minute she had de raw hide down; I give one jump out of de do', an' I saw dey came after me, but I jes' flew, and dey didn't catch me. I ran, an' I ran, an' I run, I passed many a house, but I didn't dar' to stop, for dey all knew my Missus an' dey would send me back. By an' by, when I was clar tuckered out, I come to a great big pig-pen. Dar was an ole sow dar, an' perhaps eight or ten little pigs. I was too little to climb into it, but I tumbled ober de high board, an' fell in on de ground; I was so beat out I couldn't stir.

"An' dere, Missus, I stayed from Friday till de nex' Chuesday, fightin' wid dose little pigs for de potato peelin's an" oder scraps dat came down in de trough. De ole sow would push me away when I tried to git her chillen's food, an' I was awful afeard of her. By Chuesday I was so starved I knowed I'd got to go back to my Missus, I hadn't got no whar else to go, but I knowed what was comin.' So I went back."

"And she gave you an awful flogging, I suppose, Harriet?"

"No, Missus, but *he* did."

This was all that was said, but probably that flogging left some of those scars which cover her neck and back to this day.

Think of a poor little helpless thing seven years old enduring all this terror and suffering, and yet few people are as charitable to the slave-holders as Harriet. "Dey don' know no better, Missus; it's de way dey was brought up. 'Make de little nigs min' you, or flog 'em,' was what was said to de chillen, and dey was brought up wid de whip in der hand. Now, min' you, Missus, dat wasn't de way on all de plantations; dere was good Marsters an' Missuses, as I've heard tell, but I didn't happen to come across 'em."

There is frequent mention made in the Memoir of Harriet's firm and unwavering trust in God in times of great perplexity or deadly peril, when she often had occasion to say, "Vain is the help of man, but in God is my help." I have never known another instance of such implicit trust and confidence.

Very soon after the Civil War her house was turned into a hospital, and no poor helpless creature of her race was ever turned from her door. Indeed, all through the war, and through the cruel reign of the fugitive slave law, her house was one of the depots of the "Underground Railway," as that secret and unseen mode of conveying the hunted fugitives was called, and when the war was over she established a hospital, which for many years, indeed till she was too ill herself to take charge of it, has been the refuge of the sufferers of her race who had no earthly dependence but Harriet.

Very often this woman, except for her trust in "de Lawd," had had no idea where the next meal was to come from, but she troubled herself no more about it than if she had been a Vanderbilt or an Astor. "De Lawd will provide" was her motto, and He never failed her.

One day, in passing through Auburn, I was impelled to stop over a train, and drive out to see what were the needs of my colored friend, and to take her some supplies.

Her little house was always neat and comfortable, and the small parlor was nicely and rather prettily furnished. The lame, the halt, and the blind, the bruised and crippled little children, and one crazy woman, were all brought in to see me, and "the blind woman" (she seemed to have no other name), a very old woman who had been Harriet's care for eighteen years, was led into the room — an interesting and pathetic group.

On leaving, I said to her: "If you will come out to the carriage, Harriet, there are some provisions there for you."

She turned to one of her poor dependents and said: "What did you say to me dis mornin'? You said, 'We hadn't got nothin' to eat in de house,' and what did I say to you? I said, 'I've got a rich Father!'"

Nothing that comes to this remarkable woman ever surprises her. She says very little in the way of thanks, except to the Giver of all good. How the knowledge comes to her no one can tell, but she seems always to know when help is coming, and she is generally on hand to receive it, though it is never for herself she wants it, but only for those under her care.

I must not forget to mention the Indian girls of the Fort Wrangel School, who, having read a little notice of Harriet in the "Evangelist," went to work, and by their daily labor raised thirty-seven dollars which they sent to me for Harriet — and this school has been disbanded, and these educated girls have been sent back to their wretched homes, because our Government could not afford to support it any longer!

Pundita Ramabai went about this time to see Harriet and they had an interesting talk together. Here was a remarkable trio taking hold of hands — the woman from East India, the Indian girl from the far West, and the black woman from the Southern States only two removes from an African savage!

Once when she came to New York, where she had not been in twenty years, and was starting off alone to find some friends miles away in a part of the city which she had never seen, we remonstrated with her, telling her she would surely be lost.

"Now, Missus," she said, "don't you t'ink dis ole head dat done de navigatin' down in Egypt can do de navigatin' up here in New York?"

And she walked many miles, scorning a "cyar," and found all the people she wished to see.

Harriet was known by various names among her Southern friends. One of these was "Ole Chariot," perhaps as a rhyme to the name by which they called her.

And so, often when she went to bring away a band of refugees, she would sing as she walked the dark country roads by night:

> "When dat ar' ole chariot comes,
>   Who's gwine wid me?"

And from some unseen singer would come the response:

> "When dat ar' ole chariot comes,
>   I'se gwine wid you."

And by some wireless telegraphy known only to the initiated it would be made known in one cabin or another where their deliverer was waiting concealed, and when she would be ready to pilot them on their long journey to freedom.

A Woman's Suffrage Meeting was held in Rochester a year or two ago, and Harriet came to attend it. She generally attended every meeting of women, on whatever subject, if possible to do so.

She was led into the church by an adopted daughter, whom she had rescued from death when a baby, and had brought up as her own.

The church was warm and Harriet was tired, and soon after she entered deep sleep fell upon her.

Susan B. Anthony and Mrs. Stanton were on the platform, and after speeches had been made and business accomplished, one of these ladies said:

"Friends, we have in the audience that wonderful woman, Harriet Tubman, from whom we should like to hear, if she will kindly come to the platform."

People looked around at Harriet, but Harriet was fast asleep.

"Mother! mother!" said the young girl; "they are calling for you," but it was some time before Harriet could be made to understand where she was, or what was wanted of her. At length, she was led out into the aisle and was assisted by one of these kind ladies on to the platform.

Harriet looked around, wondering why so many white ladies were gathered there. I think it was Miss Anthony who led her forward, saying:

"Ladies, I am glad to present to you Harriet Tubman, 'the conductor of the Underground Railroad.'"

"Yes, ladies," said Harriet, "I was de conductor ob de Underground Railroad for eight years, an' I can say what mos' conductors can't say — I nebber run my train off de track an' I nebber los' a passenger." The audience laughed and applauded, and Harriet was emboldened to go on and relate portions of her interesting history, which were most kindly received by the assembled ladies.

After the passage of the iniquitous fugitive slave law, Harriet removed all her dependents to Canada, and here John Brown and some of his followers took refuge with her, and she was his helper and adviser in many of his schemes. The papers of that time tell of her helping him with his plans and of his dependence upon her judgment. In one of his letters he says: "Harriet has hitched on, and with all her might; she is a whole team."

For this large party added to her own family of several persons, she worked day and night in her usual self-forgetting manner. Her old father and mother were with her, and the mother, nearly a hundred years old and enfeebled in mind, was querulous and exacting, and most unreasonable in her temper, often reproaching this faithful daughter as the Israelites did Moses of old, for "bringing them up into the wilderness to die there of hunger."

There came a day when everything eatable was exhausted, and the prospect was dark, indeed. The old mother had no tobacco and no tea — and these were more essential to her comfort than food or clothing; then reproaches thick and fast fell upon Harriet. She made no reply, but "went into her closet and shut the door"; when she came out she had a large basket on her arm.

"Catharine," she said, "take off dat small pot an' put on a large one."

"But, Harriet, der ain't not'ing in de house to eat."

"Put on de large pot, Catharine; we're gwine to have soup to-day" — and Harriet started for the market. The day was nearly over, and the market-men were anxious to be rid of their wares, and were offering them very cheap. Harriet walked along with the basket on her arm. "Old woman, don't you want a nice piece of meat?" called out one; and another, "Here's a nice piece; only ten cents. Take this soup-bone, you can have it for five cents." But Harriet had not five cents. At length a kind-hearted butcher, judging of the trouble from her face, said: "Look here, old woman, you look like an honest woman; take this soup-bone, and pay me when you get some money"; then another said, "Take this," and others piled on pieces of meat till the basket was full. Harriet passed on, and when she came to the vegetables she exchanged some of the meat for potatoes, cabbage, and onions, and the big pot was in requisition when she reached home. Harriet had not "gone into her closet and shut the door" for nothing.

I hope I may be excused for sometimes telling my story in the first person, as I cannot conveniently do it in any other way. In getting ready a Thanksgiving box to send to Harriet, a few years ago, I had ordered a turkey to be sent for it, but as the weather grew quite warm, I was advised to send a ham instead. That box was lost for three weeks, and when I saw Harriet again and told her that I had intended to send a turkey in it, she said, "Wal, dere was a clar Providence in dat, wa'n't dere, Missus?"

A friend, hearing that I was preparing a Christmas box in New York for this needy household, sent me a quantity of clothing and ten dollars for them. As my box was not quite full, I expended three dollars of that money in groceries, and sent seven dollars to a lady in Auburn who acted as treasurer for Harriet, giving her money as it was needed; for Harriet's heart is so large, and her feelings are so easily wrought upon, that it was never wise to give her more than enough for present needs.

Not long after, I received a letter from a well-known physician — a woman — in Auburn, in which she said:

"I want to tell you something about Harriet. She came to me last Friday, and said, 'Doctah, I have got my taxes and insurance to pay to-morrow, and I haven't a cent. Would you lend me seven dollars till next Chuesday?' More to try her than anything else, I said, 'Why, Harriet, I'm a poor, hard-working woman myself; how do you know you'll pay me seven dollars next Tuesday?' 'Well, Doctah, I can't jes' tell you how, but I'll pay you next Chuesday.'" On Tuesday my letter with seven dollars enclosed arrived in Auburn, and Harriet took the money to the friend who had lent it to her. Others thought this strange, but there was nothing strange about it to her.

A few years ago, when Harriet called on the writer, she was introduced to the husband of one of her daughters lately married. He told her how glad he was to see her, as he had heard so much about her. She made one of her humble courtesies, and said: "I'm pleased to see you, sir; it's de first time I've hed de pleasure makin' yo' 'quaintance since you was 'dopted into my fam'bly."

When the turns of somnolence come upon Harriet, her "sperrit," as she says, goes away from her body, and visits other scenes and places, and if she ever really sees them afterwards they are perfectly familiar to her and she can find her way about alone. Instances of this kind have lately been mentioned in some of the magazines, but Harriet had never heard of them.

Sitting in her house one day, deep sleep fell upon her, and in a dream or vision she saw a chariot in the air, going south, and empty, but soon it returned, and lying in it, cold and stiff, was the body of a young lady of whom Harriet was very fond, whose home was in Auburn, but who had gone to Washington with her father, a distinguished officer of the Government there.[9]

The shock roused Harriet from her sleep, and she ran into Auburn, to the house of her minister, crying out: "Oh, Miss Fanny is dead!" and the news had just been received.

She woke from a sleep one day in great agitation, and ran to the houses of her colored neighbors, exclaiming that "a drefful t'ing was happenin' somewha', de ground was openin', an' de houses were fallin' in, and de people bein' killed faster 'n dey was in de wah — faster 'n dey was in de wah."

At that very time, or near it, an earthquake was occurring in the northern part of South America, for the telegram came that day, though why a vision of it should be sent to Harriet no one can divine.

Her expressions are often very peculiar; some ladies of a certain church who had become interested in her wished to see her, and she was invited to come to their city, and attended the sewing circle, where twenty or thirty of them were gathered together. They asked her many questions, and she told stories, sang songs, danced, and imitated the talk of the Southern negroes; and went away loaded with many tokens of the kind interest of these ladies. On the way home she said:

"What nice, kind-lookin' ladies dem was, Missus. I looked in all dere faces, an' I didn't see nothin' venomous in one of 'em!"

As has been said, Harriet can neither read nor write; her letters are all written by an amanuensis, and she seems to have an idea that by laying her hand on this person, her feelings may be transmitted to the one to whom she is writing. These feelings are sometimes very poetically expressed. I have by me some of those letters; in one of them she says: "I lay my hand on the shoulder of the writer of this letter, and I wish for you, and all your offsprings, a through ticket in the Gospel train to Glory."

In another letter she has dictated this sentence:

"I ask of my Heavenly Father, that when the last trump sounds, and my name is called, I may stand close by your side, to answer to the call." Probably many of her friends and correspondents might contribute facts and incidents in Harriet's life quite as interesting as any I have mentioned, but I have no way of getting at them.

Harriet had long cherished the idea of having her hospital incorporated, and placed in charge of the Zion African Methodist Church of Auburn, and she was particularly anxious to come into possession of a lot of twenty-five acres of land, near her own home, to present to it as a little farm. This lot was to be sold at auction, and on the day of the sale Harriet appeared with a very little money, and a determination to have the land, cost what it might.

"Dey was all white folks but me dere, Missus, and dere I was like a blackberry in a pail ob milk, but I hid down in a corner, and no one know'd who was biddin'. De man began down pretty low, and I kept goin' up by fifties; he got up to twelve hundred, thirteen hundred, fourteen hundred, and still dat voice in the corner kept goin' up by fifties. At last it got up to fourteen hundred and fifty, an' den oders stopped biddin', an' de man said, 'All done! who is de buyer?' 'Harriet Tubman,' I shouted. 'What! dat ole nigger?' dey said. 'Old woman, how you ebber gwine to pay fer dat lot ob land?' 'I'm gwine home to tell de Lawd Jesus all about it,' I said."

After telling the Lord Jesus all about it, Harriet went down to a bank, obtained the money by mortgaging the land, and then requested to have a deed made out, making the land over to the Zion African Methodist Church. And her mind is easy about her hospital, though with many persons the trouble would be but just beginning, as there is interest on the mortgage to be paid.

Though the hospital is no longer on her hands, you will never find her without several poor creatures under her care. When I last saw her she was providing for five sick and injured ones. A blind woman came one day to her door, led by four little children — her husband had turned her out of his house, and like all other poor distressed black people, who could get there, she made her way to Harriet. Before the next morning a fifth was added to the group. As soon as it was possible Harriet dressed the whole six in white and took them to a Methodist church and had them baptized.

A little account of this was sent to the "Evangelist," and the almost immediate response was seventy-five dollars, which was of great benefit in providing for the needs of the growing family.

This faithful creature will probably not live much longer, and her like will not be seen again. But through the sale of the last edition of her "Memoir," and some other sources of income, her wants will be abundantly supplied.

Harriet's friends will be glad to learn that she has lately been for some time in Boston, where a surgical operation was performed upon her head, the skull (which was crushed by a weight thrown by her master more than seventy years before) being successfully raised. Harriet's account of this operation is rather amusing.

"Harriet," said Professor Hopkins, "what is the matter with your head? Your hair is all gone!"

"Why, dat's where dey shaved it off befo' dey cut my head open."

"Cut your head open, Harriet? What do you mean?"

"Wal, sir, when I was in Boston I walked out one day, an' I saw a great big buildin', an' I asked a man what it was, an' he said it was a hospital. So I went right in, an' I saw a young man dere, an' I said, 'Sir, are you a doctah?' an' he said he was; den I said, 'Sir, do you t'ink you could cut my head open?'

"'What do you want your head cut open fer?' he said.

"Den I tol' him de whole story, an' how my head was givin' me a powerful sight of trouble lately, with achin' an' buzzin', so I couldn' get no sleep at night.

"An' he said, 'Lay right down on dis yer table,' an' I lay down."

"Didn't he give you anything to deaden the pain, Harriet?"

"No, sir; I jes' lay down like a lamb fo' de slaughter, an' he sawed open my skull, an' raised it up, an' now it feels more comfortable." "Did you suffer very much?"

"Yes, sir, it hurt, ob cose; but I got up an' put on my bonnet an' started to walk home, but my legs kin o' gin out under me, an' dey sont fer a ambulance an' sont me home."

It has been hoped that this remarkable experience might result in giving Harriet a new lease of life, but I am sorry to say she is very feeble, and I fear will not be with us much longer.

Her "through ticket" has long been ready for her, and when her last journey is accomplished can we doubt that she will be welcomed to one of those many mansions prepared for those who have spent their lives in the Master's service?

APPENDIX

The following letters to the writer from those well-known and distinguished philanthropists, Hon. Gerrit Smith and Wendell Phillips, and one from Frederick Douglass, addressed to Harriet, will serve as the best introduction that can be given of the subject of this memoir to its readers:

Letter from Hon. Gerrit Smith.

PETERBORO, *June* 13, 1868.

MY DEAR MADAME: I am happy to learn that you are to speak to the public of Mrs. Harriet Tubman. Of the remarkable events of her life I have no *personal* knowledge, but of the truth of them as she describes them I have no doubt.

I have often listened to her, in her visits to my family, and I am confident that she is not only truthful, but that she has a rare discernment, and a deep and sublime philanthropy.

With great respect your friend,

GERRIT SMITH.

Letter from Wendell Phillips.

June 16, 1868.

DEAR MADAME: The last time I ever saw John Brown was under my own roof, as he brought Harriet Tubman to me, saying: "Mr. Phillips, I bring you one of the best and bravest persons on this continent — *General* Tubman, as we call her."

He then went on to recount her labors and sacrifices in behalf of her race. After that, Harriet spent some time in Boston, earning the confidence and admiration of all those who were working for freedom. With their aid she went to the South more than once, returning always with a squad of self-emancipated men, women, and children, for whom her marvelous skill had opened the way of escape. After the war broke out, she was sent with indorsements from Governor Andrew and his friends to South Carolina, where in the service of the Nation she rendered most important and efficient aid to our army.

In my opinion there are few captains, perhaps few colonels, who have done more for the loyal cause since the war began, and few men who did before that time more for the colored race, than our fearless and most sagacious friend, Harriet.

Faithfully yours,

WENDELL PHILLIPS.

Letter from Frederick Douglass.

ROCHESTER, *August* 29, 1868.

DEAR HARRIET: I am glad to know that the story of your eventful life has been written by a kind lady, and that the same is soon to be published. You ask for what you do not need when you call upon me for a word of commendation. I need such words from you far more than you can need them from me, especially where your superior labors and devotion to the cause of the lately enslaved of our land are known as I know them. The difference between us is very marked. Most that I have done and suffered in the service of our cause has been in public, and I have received much encouragement at every step of the way. You, on the other hand, have labored in a private way. I have wrought in the day — you in the night. I have had the applause of the crowd and the satisfaction that comes of being approved by the multitude, while the most that you have done has been witnessed by a few trembling, scarred, and foot-sore bondmen and women, whom you have led out of the house of bondage, and whose heartfelt "*God bless you*" has been your only reward. The midnight sky and the silent stars have been the witnesses of your devotion to freedom and of your heroism. Excepting John Brown — of sacred memory — I know of no one who has willingly encountered more perils and hardships to serve our enslaved people than you have. Much that you have done would seem improbable to those who do not know you as I know you. It is to me a great pleasure and a great privilege to bear testimony to your character and your works, and to say to those to whom you may come, that I regard you in every way truthful and trustworthy.

Your friend,

FREDERICK DOUGLASS.

Extracts from a Letter written by Mr. Sanborn, Secretary of the Massachusetts Board of State Charities.

MY DEAR MADAME: Mr. Phillips has sent me your note, asking for reminiscences of Harriet Tubman, and testimonials to her extraordinary story, which all her New England friends will, I am sure, be glad to furnish.

I never had reason to doubt the truth of what Harriet said in regard to her own career, for I found her singularly truthful. Her imagination is warm and rich, and there is a whole region of the marvelous in her nature, which has manifested itself at times remarkably. Her dreams and visions, misgivings and forewarnings, ought not to be omitted in any life of her, particularly those relating to John Brown.

She was in his confidence in 1858-9, and he had a great regard for her, which he often expressed to me. She aided him in his plans, and expected to do so still further, when his career was closed by that wonderful campaign in Virginia. The first time she came to my house, in Concord, after that tragedy, she was shown into a room in the evening, where Brackett's bust of John Brown was standing. The sight of it, which was new to her, threw her into a sort of ecstacy of sorrow and admiration, and she went on in her rhapsodical way to pronounce his apotheosis.

She has often been in Concord, where she resided at the houses of Emerson, Alcott, the Whitneys, the Brooks family, Mrs. Horace Mann, and other well-known persons. They all admired and respected her, and nobody doubted the reality of her adventures. She was too *real* a person to be suspected. In 1862, I think it was, she went from Boston to Port Royal, under the advice and encouragement of Mr. Garrison, Governor Andrew, Dr. Howe, and other leading people. Her career in South Carolina is well known to some of our officers, and I think to Colonel Higginson, now of Newport, R.I., and Colonel James Montgomery, of Kansas, to both of whom she was useful as a spy and guide, if I mistake not. I regard her as, on the whole, the most extraordinary person of her race I have ever met. She is a negro of pure, or almost pure blood, can neither read nor write, and has the characteristics of her race and condition. But she has done what can scarcely be credited on the best authority, and she has accomplished her purposes with a coolness, foresight, patience and wisdom, which in a *white man* would have raised him to the highest pitch of reputation.

I am, dear Madame, very truly your servant,

F.B. SANBORN.

Letter from Hon. Wm.H. Seward.

WASHINGTON, *July* 25, 1868.

MAJ.-GEN. HUNTER —

MY DEAR SIR: Harriet Tubman, a colored woman, has been nursing our soldiers during nearly all the war. She believes she has a claim for faithful services to the command in South Carolina with which you are connected, and she thinks that you would be disposed to see her claim justly settled.

I have known her long, and a nobler, higher spirit, or a truer, seldom dwells in the human form. I commend her, therefore, to your kind and best attentions.

Faithfully your friend,

WILLIAM H. SEWARD.

Letter from Col. James Montgomery.

ST. HELENA ISLAND, S.C., *July* 6, 1863.

HEADQUARTERS COLORED BRIGADE.

BRIG.-GEN. GILMORE, Commanding Department of the South —

GENERAL: I wish to commend to your attention, Mrs. Harriet Tubman, a most remarkable woman, and invaluable as a scout. I have been acquainted with her character and actions for several years.

I am, General, your most ob't servant,

JAMES MONTGOMERY, Col. Com. Brigade.

Letter from Mrs. Gen. A. Baird.

PETERBORO, *Nov.* 24, 1864.

The bearer of this, Harriet Tubman, a most excellent woman, who has rendered faithful and good services to our Union army, not only in the hospital, but in various capacities, having been employed under Government at Hilton Head, and in Florida; and I commend her to the protection of all officers in whose department she may happen to be.

She has been known and esteemed for years by the family of my uncle, Hon. Gerrit Smith, as a person of great rectitude and capabilities.

MRS. GEN. A. BAIRD.

Letter from Hon. Gerrit Smith.

PETERBORO, N.Y., *Nov.* 4, 1867.

I have known Mrs. Harriet Tubman for many years. Seldom, if ever, have I met with a person more philanthropic, more self-denying, and of more bravery. Nor must I omit to say that she combines with her sublime spirit, remarkable discernment and judgment.

During the late war, Mrs. Tubman was eminently faithful and useful to the cause of our country. She is poor and has poor parents. Such a servant of the country should be well paid by the country. I hope that the Government will look into her case.

GERRIT SMITH.

Testimonial from Gerrit Smith.

PETERBORO, *Nov.* 22, 1864.

The bearer, Harriet Tubman, needs not any recommendation. Nearly all the nation over, she has been heard of for her wisdom, integrity, patriotism, and bravery. The cause of freedom owes her much. The country owes her much.

I have known Harriet for many years, and I hold her in my high esteem.

GERRIT SMITH.

Certificate from Henry K. Durrant, Acting Asst. Surgeon, U.S.A.

I certify that I have been acquainted with Harriet Tubman for nearly two years; and my position as Medical Officer in charge of "contrabands" in this town and in hospital, has given me frequent and ample opportunities to observe her general deportment; particularly her kindness and attention to the sick and suffering of her own race. I take much pleasure in testifying to the esteem in which she is generally held.

HENRY K. DURRANT,
Acting Assistant Surgeon, U. S. A.

In charge "Contraband" Hospital.

Dated at Beaufort, S.C., the 3d day of May, 1864.
I concur fully in the above.

R. SAXTON, Brig.-Gen. Vol.

The following are a few of the passes used by Harriet throughout the war. Many others are so defaced that it is impossible to decipher them.

HEADQUARTERS DEPARTMENT OF THE SOUTH,

HILTON HEAD, PORT ROYAL, S.C., *Feb.* 19, 1863.

Pass the bearer, Harriet Tubman, to Beaufort and back to this place, and wherever she wishes to go; and give her free passage at all times, on all Government transports. Harriet was sent to me from Boston by Governor Andrew, of Massachusetts, and is a valuable woman. She has permission, as a servant of the Government, to purchase such provisions from the Commissary as she may need.

D. HUNTER, Maj.-Gen. Com.

General Gilmore, who succeeded General Hunter in command of the Department of the South, appends his signature to the same pass.

HEADQUARTERS OF THE DEPARTMENT OF THE SOUTH,
July 1, 1863.

Continued in force.

Q.A. GILMORE, Brig.-Gen. Com.

BEAUFORT, *Aug.* 28, 1862.

Will Capt. Warfield please let "Moses" have a little Bourbon whiskey for medicinal purposes.

HENRY K. DURANT, Act. Ass. Surgeon.

WAR DEPARTMENT, WASHINGTON, D. C,
March 20, 1865.

Pass Mrs. Harriet Tubman (colored) to Hilton Head and Charleston, S.C., with free transportation on a Government transport,

By order of the Sec. of War.
Louis H., Asst. Adj.-Gen., U.S.A.
To Bvt. Brig.-Gen. Van Vliet, U.S.Q.M., N.Y.
Not transferable.

WAR DEPARTMENT, WASHINGTON, D.C.,
July 22, 1865.

Permit Harriet Tubman to proceed to Fortress Monroe, Va., on a Government transport. Transportation will be furnished free of cost.

By order of the Secretary of War.
L.H., Asst. Adj.-Gen.
Not transferable.

Appointment as Nurse.

SIR: I have the honor to inform you that the Medical Director Department of Virginia has been instructed to appoint Harriet Tubman nurse or matron at the Colored Hospital, Fort Monroe, Va.

> Very respectfully, your obdt. servant,
> V.K. BARNES, Surgeon-General.
> Hon. WM.H. SEWARD,
> Secretary of State, Washington, D.C.

Of the many letters, testimonials, and passes, placed in the hands of the writer by Harriet, the following are selected for insertion in this book, and are quite sufficient to verify her statements.

A Letter from Gen. Saxton to a lady of Auburn.

ATLANTA, GA., *March* 21, 1868.

MY DEAR MADAME: I have just received your letter informing me that Hon. Wm.H. Seward, Secretary of State, would present a petition to Congress for a pension to Harriet Tubman, for services rendered in the Union Army during the late war. I can bear witness to the value of her services in South Carolina and Florida. She was employed in the hospitals and as a spy. She made many a raid inside the enemy's lines, displaying remarkable courage, zeal, and fidelity. She was employed by General Hunter, and I think by Generals Stevens and Sherman, and is as deserving of a pension from the Government for her services as any other of its faithful servants.

I am very truly yours,

RUFUS SAXTON, Bvt. Brig.-Gen., U.S.A.

Rev. Samuel I. May, in his recollections of the anti-slavery conflict, after mentioning the case of an old slave mother, whom he vainly endeavored to assist her son in buying from her master, says:
"I did not until four years after know that remarkable woman Harriet, or I might have engaged her services, in the assurance that she would have bought off the old woman without *paying* for her inalienable right — her liberty."
Mr. May in another place says of Harriet, that she deserves to be placed *first* on the list of American heroines, and then proceeds to give a short account of her labors, varying very little from that given in this book.

FUGITIVE SLAVE RESCUE IN TROY

From the *Troy Whig*, April 28, 1859.

Yesterday afternoon, the streets of this city and West Troy were made the scenes of unexampled excitement. For the first time since the passage of the Fugitive Slave Law, an attempt was made here to carry its provisions into execution, and the result was a terrific encounter between the officers and the prisoner's friends, the triumph of mob law, and the final rescue of the fugitive. Our city was thrown into a grand state of turmoil, and for a time every other topic was forgotten, to give place to this new excitement. People did not think last evening to ask who was nominated at Charleston, or whether the news of the Heenan and Sayers battle had arrived — everything was merged into the fugitive slave case, of which it seems the end is not yet.

Charles Nalle, the fugitive, who was the cause of all this excitement, was a slave on the plantation of B.W. Hansborough, in Culpepper County, Virginia, till the 19th of October, 1858, when he made his escape, and went to live in Columbia, Pennsylvania. A wife and five children are residing there now. Not long since he came to Sandlake, in this county, and resided in the family of Mr. Crosby until about three weeks ago. Since that time, he has been employed as coachman by Uri Gilbert, Esq., of this city. He is about thirty years of age, tall, quite light-complexioned, and good-looking. He is said to have been an excellent and faithful servant.

At Sandlake, we understand that Nalle was often seen by one H.F. Averill, formerly connected with one of the papers of this city, who communicated with his reputed owner in Virginia, and gave the information that led to a knowledge of the whereabouts of the fugitive. Averill wrote letters for him, and thus obtained an acquaintance with his history. Mr. Hansborough sent on an agent, Henry J. Wall, by whom the necessary papers were got out to arrest the fugitive.

Yesterday morning about 11 o'clock, Charles Nalle was sent to procure some bread for the family by whom he was employed. He failed to return. At the baker's he was arrested by Deputy United States Marshal J.W. Holmes, and immediately taken before United States Commissioner Miles Beach. The son of Mr. Gilbert, thinking it strange that he did not come back, sent to the house of William Henry, on Division Street, where he boarded, and his whereabouts was discovered.

The examination before Commissioner Beach was quite brief. The evidence of Averill and the agent was taken, and the Commissioner decided to remand Nalle to Virginia. The necessary papers were made out and given to the Marshal.

By this time it was two o'clock, and the fact began to be noised abroad that there was a fugitive slave in Mr. Beach's office, corner of State and First Streets. People in knots of ten or twelve collected near the entrance, looking at Nalle, who could be seen at an upper window. William Henry, a colored man, with whom Nalle boarded, commenced talking from the curb-stone in a loud voice to the crowd. He uttered such sentences as, "There is a fugitive slave in that office — pretty soon you will see him come forth. He is going to be taken down South, and you will have a chance to see him. He is to be taken to the depot, to go to Virginia in the first train. Keep watch of those stairs, and you will have a sight." A number of women kept shouting, crying, and by loud appeals excited the colored persons assembled.

Still the crowd grew in numbers. Wagons halted in front of the locality, and were soon piled with spectators. An alarm of fire was sounded, and hose carriages dashed through the ranks of men, women, and boys; but they closed again, and kept looking with expectant eyes at the window where the negro was visible. Meanwhile, angry discussions commenced. Some persons agitated a rescue, and others favored law and order. Mr. Brockway, a lawyer, had his coat torn for expressing his sentiments, and other *mêlées* kept the interest alive.

All at once there was a wild halloo, and every eye was turned up to see the legs and part of the body of the prisoner protruding from the second story window, at which he was endeavoring to escape. Then arose a shout! "Drop him!" "Catch him!" "Hurrah!" But the attempt was a fruitless one, for somebody in the office pulled Nalle back again, amid the shouts of a hundred pairs of lungs. The crowd at this time numbered nearly a thousand persons. Many of them were black, and a good share were of the female sex. They blocked up State Street from First Street to the alley, and kept surging to and fro.

Martin I. Townsend, Esq., who acted as counsel for the fugitive, did not arrive in the Commissioner's office until a decision had been rendered. He immediately went before Judge Gould, of the Supreme Court, and procured a writ of habeas corpus in the usual form, *returnable* immediately. This was given Deputy-Sheriff Nathaniel Upham, who at once proceeded to Commissioner Beach's office, and served it on Holmes. Very injudiciously, the officers proceeded at once to Judge Gould's office, although it was evident they would have to pass through an excited, unreasonable crowd. As soon as the officers and their prisoner emerged from the door, an old negro, who had been standing at the bottom of the stairs, shouted, "Here they come," and the crowd made a terrific rush at the party.

From the office of Commissioner Beach, in the Mutual Building, to that of Judge Gould, in Congress Street, is less than two blocks, but it was made a regular battlefield. The moment the prisoner emerged from the doorway, in custody of Deputy-Sheriff Upham, Chief of Police Quin, Officers Cleveland and Holmes, the crowd made one grand charge, and those nearest the prisoner seized him violently, with the intention of pulling him away from the officers, but they were foiled; and down First to Congress Street, and up the latter in front of Judge Gould's chambers, went the surging mass. Exactly what did go on in the crowd, it is impossible to say, but the pulling, hauling, mauling, and shouting, gave evidences of frantic efforts on the part of the rescuers, and a stern resistance from the conservators of the law. In front of Judge Gould's office the combat was at its height. No stones or other missiles were used; the battle was fist to fist. We believe an order was given to take the prisoner the other way, and there was a grand rush towards the West, past First and River Streets, as far as Dock Street. All this time there was a continual *mêlée*. Many of the officers were hurt — among them Mr. Upham, whose object was solely to do his duty by taking Nalle before Judge Gould in accordance with the writ of habeas corpus. A number in the crowd were more or less hurt, and it is a wonder that these were not badly injured, as pistols were drawn and chisels used.

The battle had raged as far as the corner of Dock and Congress Streets, and the victory remained with the rescuers at last. The officers were completely worn out with their exertions, and it was impossible to continue their hold upon him any longer. Nalle was at liberty. His friends rushed him down Dock Street to the lower ferry, where there was a skiff lying ready to start. The fugitive was put in, the ferryman rowed off, and amid the shouts of hundreds who lined the banks of the river, Nalle was carried into Albany County.

As the skiff landed in West Troy, a negro sympathizer waded up to the waist, and pulled Nalle out of the boat. He went up the hill alone, however, and there who should he meet but Constable Becker! The latter official seeing a man with manacles on, considered it his duty to arrest him. He did so, and took him in a wagon to the office of Justice Stewart, on the second floor of the corner building near the ferry. The justice was absent.

When the crowd on the Troy bank had seen Nalle safely landed, it was suggested that he might be recaptured. Then there was another rush made for the steam ferry-boat, which carried over about 400 persons, and left as many more — a few of the latter being soused in their efforts to get on the boat. On landing in West Troy, there, sure enough, was the prisoner, locked up in a strong office, protected by Officers Becker, Brown and Morrison, and the door barricaded.

Not a moment was lost. Up stairs went a score or more of resolute men — the rest "piling in" promiscuously, shouting and execrating the officers. Soon a stone flew against the door — then another — and bang, bang! went off a couple of pistols, but the officers who fired them took good care to aim pretty high. The assailants were forced to retreat for a moment. "They've got pistols," said one. "Who cares?" was the reply; "they can only kill a dozen of us — come on." More stones and more pistol-shots ensued. At last the door was pulled open by an immense negro, and in a moment he was felled by a hatchet in the hands of Deputy-Sheriff Morrison; but the body of the fallen man blocked up the door so that it could not be shut, and a friend of the prisoner pulled him out. Poor fellow! he might well say, "Save me from my friends." Amid the pulling and hauling, the iron had cut his arms, which were bleeding profusely, and he could hardly walk, owing to fatigue.

He has since arrived safely in Canada.